SELF-HARM

Perspectives from Personal Experience

Edited by Louise Roxanne Pembroke

www.chipmunkapublishing.com

First Edition, October 1994
Reprinted, April 1995
Revised and reprinted, October 1996
Reprinted 2004

© Survivors Speak Out

ISBN 1-904697-04-6

Layout and cover illustration designed and set by David Crepaz-Keay, Andy Smith and Louise Roxanne Pembroke for Survivors Speak Out.

Canterbury College

CONTENTS

Dedication

This book is dedicated to Maggy Ross, a survivor of self-harm, sexual abuse and psychiatric treatment. She was one of the founder members of the Bristol Crisis Service for Women and she campaigned passionately and eloquently during her life for a greater understanding of self-harm. She wanted to make it better for others turning to self-harm in the future. She died in her struggle, but it is because of people like Maggy that others became empowered to stand up and speak out. Maggy knew that whenever a person gained their voice, it is a victory for all of us. That each time a person is incarcerated it is an indictment of our society, not their mental state. We are indebted to her.

INTRODUCTION

Self-Harm is as taboo as sexual abuse has been. For those who live with it there is much fear and shame in talking about it. For those who work with self-harm there is great reluctance to face it beyond the stereotype. What remains is a huge gulf which is allowing thousands of people to be abused and humiliated by the medical and psychiatric services. This situation reinforces societies socialisation of women which encourages self-harm. That encourages all of us to be controlled and controlling. We straitjacket our feelings, perceptions and bodies to our detriment because society values it and society permits a narrow range of expressions of distress. To be driven, quite literally, to tearing our bodies apart and having to endure services which compound the problem speaks volumes about how expressions of human pain are categorised. To cry or fade away quietly is easier for others to bear, but to see someone tear themselves apart appears incomprehensible and revolting. Self-harm is a painful but understandable response to distress, particularly in western culture. Self-harm thrives in an environment where people are stripped of freedom and control over their lives and yet are expected to behave in a controlled manner. (Prisons, Special Hospitals, psychiatric hospitals, Local Authority care for young people, etc). Self-harm is a sane response when people are gagged in order to maintain the social order. Self-harm mirrors what we don't want to acknowledge. Explosive feelings implode. Our emotional corset cannot hold the pain in any longer, so it busts. Self-harm is about self-worth, self-preservation, lack of choices, and coping with the uncopeable. To quote Maggy Ross who spoke at the first national self-harm conference in 1989;

"It is about trying to create a sense of order out of chaos. It's a visual manifestation of extreme distress".

There are some common precipitating factors - sexual abuse, eating distress or psychiatric incarceration, but these factors are by no means universal. The roots and manifestations of this distress can be diverse and complex. There are no rigid 'personality types'. There is not one 'group' of 'symptoms'.

Self-harm attracts little research interest. Existing research reinforces the typical pejorative stereotypes; *"maladaptive"*, *"deviant"*, *"a reduced capacity to regulate affect"*, *"immature responses"*, *"manipulative"*, and even, *"passive problem solving style"*. It is hard to see how self-mutilation could possibly be viewed as *"passive"*.

Responses to self-harm are predominantly negative and punitive. Some of the suggested "therapeutic" techniques make me want to reach for the nearest packet of razor blades. People with direct experience and women's organisations concerned about self-injury would disagree with many of the strange conclusions that have been drawn.

1

In one paper, a psychiatrist suggests that there are three types of self-cutting ranging from superficial cutting which is supposedly associated with little or no suicidal intent. Through to self-mutilation that results in disfigurement, and is supposedly more likely to occur in individuals with so-called 'psychotic illness'. This equates to alleging there are only three ways of breaking your leg, thus missing the point. In common with attempted suicide, the yardstick used for measuring risk and intent is often the resulting degree of injury or illness. The intent in self-cutting may bear little or no relation to the resulting injury. The feelings may be the same, whether the result is a scratch or a laceration to the bone. These categorisations serve only to trivialise the 'lesser' injuries whilst leaving the more 'serious' injuries equally condemned to another stereotype. The reasons, motivation and intent for all types of self-harm are as diverse as the reasons for attempted suicide.

Self-harm and language used to describe it.

There are two distinct types of self-harm;

Firstly, self-harm with suicidal intent (or attempted suicide).

Secondly, self-harm without suicidal intent. This embraces a broad spectrum of behaviour.

This range includes all of us, but it is the less socially acceptable forms of self-harm this book examines.

The second category of self-harm (non-suicidal) may lead to a suicide attempt but, in itself, is usually quite the opposite. An attempt at self-preservation. Socially acceptable forms of self-harm include; excessive smoking, drinking, exercise, liposuction, bikini-line waxing, high heels and body piercing. Western societies endorse and promote women's assaults on their bodies by dieting. This form of self-harm is encouraged by cultural and gender expectations and pressures. More women die in the United States as a result of eating distress than of A.I.D.S.

The socially acceptable range of self-harm clearly does not include; self-cutting, burning, smashing bones and pouring toxic substances over or into our bodies. This is normally referred to by the medical profession as self-mutilation, more commonly, 'Deliberate Self-Harm' (D.S.H.). Deliberate Self-Harm is applied to all cases of self-harm ignoring the intent. The term 'Deliberate Self-Harm' is objectionable. 'Deliberate' can imply premeditation and wilfulness. Self-harm is always atypical. Sometimes it can be spontaneous and sudden with little awareness or conscious thought. Conversely, the drive to self-harm maybe powerfully constant and unrelenting with a conscious battle raging. How self-harm occurs and the levels of awareness vary considerably. Self-harm or self-injury does not require qualifying with **'Deliberate'**. Some forms of self-harm don't have the social seal of approval. It is denied as an expression of distress. It goes against the pre-occupation with maintaining 'beauty' and achieving some perceived image of 'perfection'. We all harm ourselves to a certain extent to keep ourselves nice, neat and calm. We mustn't get angry! Health services and workers often recoil from self-harmers, occasionally to the point of medical negligence. Health services are not geared towards people who need to damage themselves. We appear to be destroying ourselves contrary to the services' aim to preserve life. Self-harm mirrors painful or destructive elements they do not want to recognise in themselves, their profession and in the world around them. It's a bit too close to the bone...

The N.H.S. rationalising will result in further marginalisation and degradation of people who self-harm. When resources are limited and services defined by finance as opposed to need, self-harm looks expendable. Smokers have been refused treatment for smoking-related illnesses. It's self-inflicted. I have been refused essential treatment for an injury. Told that I should not be treated anymore as there was no point. It was self-inflicted and would happen again. It wasn't worth it. I was not worth healing. As financial pressures will force doctors to choose who gets treatment, presenting moral judgement in the guise of clinical judgement will be easier. Medical treatment should be a **right**, not something that has to be deserved. That is health fascism.

It is common to be stitched with no or inadequate anaesthesia, not having each layer of tissue properly stitched, being used as training material or having observers present without consent. These practices are widespread and must stop. **Now**. Complaints are difficult and rare, self-harmers usually feel that they will not be believed, and that a complaint would make future treatment worse or inaccessible. No amount of 'Patient Charters' will help us. Men and women express the same feelings about psychiatric 'help'. They are not listened to, dismissed and written off. The favoured treatment is crude behaviourist techniques. As Phillip Hutchinson, a psychiatric survivor observed, *"The greatest condemnation of psychiatry is that some of us would rather be on the brink of destruction than accept what they offer as 'help'"*

The only way forward is to end the silence. For people with direct experience to share their experiences, and for a dialogue to start between self-harmers and service agencies. Then there is a need for greater mutual understanding and professional assumptions must be surrendered if the current figure of 100,000 people being treated annually for self-inflicted injuries is to be reduced.

As Mike Lawson, former Vice-Chair of MIND has said, *"The greatest asset we have for change is our voices and our ears"*.

For the first time at the self-harm conference of 1989, male and female survivors of self-harm and treatment came together to speak in a way that is not usually heard. They gave accounts of their experiences and analyses of treatments and orthodox theories. They set out the agenda, the problems and guidance for approaching this subject with more humanity. Three of the contributions in this book are speeches from that conference. For some of the health and mental health workers present at the conference, listening to the survivors brought about a U-turn of their feelings towards self-harm. One woman stood up and stated she had been taught that self-harm was always "attention-seeking". On realising that this was not the case she announced her intention to leave her job as she could not continue to work from that framework of belief. It was clear that when survivors and workers listened to one another, there was much to be gained.

Public awareness of self-harm is growing and this book is intended to aid that growing awareness of the problems we encounter. This is essential reading for anyone who has been through self-harm and those who work with us. It is relevant to anyone who has ever wanted to look beyond "Attention-Seeking".

To see the person behind the scars.

DIANE HARRISON

Glad to be asked to share my experiences with you.

I feel quite nervous and I want to say why it's hard to talk - I am an incest survivor, my family didn't encourage disclosure of problems and feelings. To have talked would have meant punishment, I was even threatened with death for speaking out.

It's been hard for me to believe I matter to anyone, least of all myself. Years of struggle without anyone seeming to notice or to care about me and who I am. I often tortured myself just to feel something and to make anyone notice me. Even then I've believed they've only wanted to clean up my wounds to make me appear more acceptable on the outside. Inside I felt cut up to tiny pieces. I have had years of therapy to bring me to this point - the point in time where I have no more secrets and I **will** speak out.

Mine was a secret life, shared only with my grandfather who abused me - I loved him but learnt love went with punishment - pleasure with pain until I was lost in confusion. No one wanted to know. They said I was an imaginative child and I believed them, I believed it was all my doing. Inside myself I was in prison for a crime I couldn't understand - **except that I was guilty.**

Inside I wanted to scream but dare not do so to anyone for my own survival. I feared my mother would leave home as she'd threatened to do before, and I'd die in the hands of my grandfather. I wanted to change it somehow, I wanted to be good so someone would notice and give me attention. I needed attention - I was less than 5 years old. I remember myself as a little tot, I enjoyed dancing and singing in front of my relatives. No-one noticed that this small individual stopped dancing and singing. Instead I learnt to act differently, I played along with them and kept my real self secret, so secret that I became lost.

I'd like to read you a poem I wrote in therapy and which I've included in the autobiography I'm writing:

The Child.

All screwed up in a corner,
Like a tight little ball
Hiding in the darkness,
The child awaits - what?

Memories of fear,
The child can't forget
The consequences
Of being found - needing.

Stay hidden, stay hidden!
Swallow the pain and dirt
Till it goes downwards, deeper
Hidden and lost - inside.

Emerge with a smile
Yes, everything's fine!
For nature numbs agony
The child **must** survive.

By the time I was 7 I was punching and scratching myself with twigs. I had so much inside that I wanted to get rid of. I remember screaming into the pillow at night, scared that someone would hear.

I was protecting my mother from my feelings because she couldn't cope with me. I also knew that I'd have been punished and not believed. I got headaches every fortnight which brought some sympathy from my mother, who incidentally suffered from them herself. Physical hurt she could cope with. These were the only times we communicated on a more sharing level.

By 11 I was cutting myself with razors, saying that I'd had an accident or not saying anything at all. I could cope with this type of pain, it took away the horrible feelings I had inside for a short while. I could even begin to love my wounds. I had control over the pain, over something in my life which strangely felt good.

After an overdose at 16 I left home. My grandfather had died the year before, leaving me thinking I was pregnant. As I knew pain, I used knitting needles to give myself an abortion, and later thinking myself wicked, tried to commit suicide. No-one really looked into why, no-one had known of the feared pregnancy. Whom could I talk to? No-one, so I ran away from my home and from my head. After this I completely blanked out my past.

I became a nurse at 18. Oh yes, I was a capable, responsible nurse. Always laughing and jolly. I did well convincing everyone that I was fine, I even convinced myself most of the time. But when things built up and I found it hard to put on the act, I injured myself by injecting dirty substances into my body causing abscesses that had to be drained. I had reason then to look low. I'd had another accident hadn't I?

I feared being labelled mentally ill, anyway it was my guilty secret though I didn't know why I was doing it. I just had to stop feeling any mental pain.

I would unconsciously destroy everything in my life that was good: relationships or friendships. I was scared to let anyone get close, to risk their rejection. I felt dirty inside, unlovable. I got married and had three children but my marriage broke up. This was a lot to do with my difficulties. My husband didn't physically hurt me, but in a way I wanted him to, I couldn't believe in love unless I felt pain.

Some time later I had a road accident, this was the final straw and my past surfaced one day when I was with my social worker. I had 6 weeks of counselling with her and then went on to find a therapist.

Because I wasn't able to cope with the feelings therapy was bringing up and my children too, I started cutting myself again, took Paracetomol, began to drink and became Bulimic. My therapist often got angry with my behaviour but I was coping in the only way I knew how. I didn't want to hurt my children so took it out on myself.

In retrospect I was also reliving past hurt, re-feeling the emotional pain because I hadn't been able to work through, or come to terms with it. I tortured myself over and over again.

My children were eventually taken to live with their father, where they still are and I went in and out of psychiatric hospital many times.

I was often taken to casualty with throat injuries I'd inflicted on myself, or Paracetomol overdoses. I was always treated in the same way;

"Why did you do it?"

"This is making it worse".

"We're very busy in here".

"You must see a psychiatrist - if you don't and you come back here again this will all have been a waste of our time".

It was all questions when there were no simple answers. It was too hard to speak, I was scared of being punished, and I often was. They'd leave me to get on with it, or to pull myself together. I needed someone to listen, or just to be with me if there were no words for how I felt. The staff often got angry which made me feel useless and suicidal, then I would take another, much larger overdose, or try to cut an artery.

The hospital staff by their attitude of non-acceptance of my pain, reinforced these feelings. I was only acceptable if I acted in the way they wanted me to behave. Negativity being unacceptable, having a positive attitude is good and is given the reward of attention.

In the end I lost my home, I couldn't cope with living in the same house that I'd lived in with my children. By this time I was terribly Bulimic, and weighed less than half my original weight. I had no support given to me and was too ill to be able to get to my therapist. In between binges I swallowed glass, drank or took more Paracetomol. I just wanted to take the pain away, even if it had killed me - I didn't care and no-one else seemed to.

After my next admission I found out about, and then moved into, a single women's supportive hostel where I received twice weekly counselling. For some time I continued to self-injure. I couldn't believe anyone was listening to me. I was waiting to be punished and rejected - but wasn't.

No-one blamed me. They accepted me however I was and although it was a struggle, I began to slowly care about myself and my life. I was at last being listened to, every part of me. Both good and what I thought was bad being given attention. I look back now and realise I needed to be mothered in order to grow and to find myself. It was like going back into the womb, finding a safe place to be. I lived there for 2 years. It was an essential part of my journey. A warm, resting, growing place.

I joined the setting up group of the Women's Crisis Service in Bristol and for the first time in my life met other women who self-injured. I no longer felt a freak, I found some people who understood because they shared similar experiences.

We opened our weekend women's telephone help-line in 1988, which is run by women volunteers, working on Friday and Saturday evenings. We found that it was important to have a service open to women only, to give them a sense of safety in being listened to by another woman. We offer support over the phone, letting women express their problems and feelings in supporting acceptance, helping them to work through it.

We counsel many women, some of whom ring in from various parts of the country, but we don't only support women who self-injure as in cutting, nor do all our volunteers have this experience. We listen to various crisis or emotional problems from loneliness and depression, to eating disorders or drug addictions. We've learnt that we all share similar concerns. Every one of us is capable of self-injuring in some way when feeling out of balance with ourselves.

Sadly, we've also learnt that there is little in the way of help available to women, especially those who can least afford to pay for it. We now do talks and workshops locally and around the country.

I'd like to end with a poem I wrote as I came through therapy. Dedicated to anyone whom has contact with or helps anyone who self-injures.

See me.

See me,
Who do you see?
Is it the smiling face?
Is it the person
Who confidently tells you
That her life is well intact?

Don't worry,
I won't tell you,
You've no need to fear that I will crumble
In front of you.
Your eyes tell me
That you don't really want to know.
So why should I make myself
That vulnerable?
- Never.

See me,
Who do you see?
The person beneath
That surface calm
Hides from you.

Your rejection or punishment
I couldn't stand
So my mind runs
From my body in sadness
Mingled now
With anger and rage.
I reject myself
And take up the knife

Plunge into innocent flesh
Till the blood runs out
Washing away the anger and pain
- Till the next time.

See me,
Who do I see?
Yet another person
Who tries to help
By daring to look inside me.

I have to trust you first though,
Enough to let you into
My abused body
And make myself that vulnerable
All over again
To someone else
Who calls themself my Therapist or friend?

See me,
Who do you see?
I trust you more now
As times gone by
But I still fear your rejection.

Now, don't make me reward you
By good behaviour
For I still want to cut out my sin.
Just who feels better
If I don't self-injure?
Not me, only you
And I want you to - **like me**
- So I do it in secret, instead.

See me
Who do you see?
A person who grows stronger
But I still feel caught up

In the past
Fearing new ways of being me.

I slip back
When it all gets too much
And hurt myself some more.
But don't punish me for that
Don't you hurt yourself too?
I show you my scars
But yours are hidden from me.
You tell me you're tired,
Been working too hard?
Up late last night?
Smoking or drinking?
And why were you off sick last week?
Does this not reflect
Like a mirror
The state of **your** mind?

So who's supporting you?
Listening and accepting the good and bad
Feelings that we all have.
I know and own mine
- But do you?

Will you not accept
Them in yourself?
And learn to express them
In other ways
Than by hurting yourself
Or getting angry at me?

See me,
See **you**,
Do I not reflect
An image of yourself
- The one **you cannot stand?**

PROFESSIONAL THOUGHT DISORDER PART I:
(The staff nurse seriously overestimates her intellect).

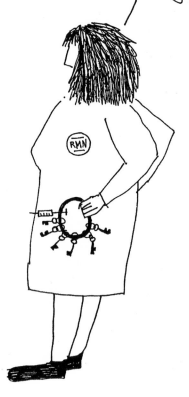

MAGGY ROSS

I'm Maggy and I started to cut my body 5 years ago.

It all started innocently enough. I was sitting in the sun outside a psychiatric hospital and noticed some glass glinting in the sunlight. I picked up a piece and started to cut the back of my hand. Since then I've used broken wine glasses, knives, scalpels, even a watch buckle. I then 'progressed' to razor blades. I've cut my arms, face and right leg. The left leg remains untouched - its important to me that one part of me remains scar-free. Don't ask me why!

When I cut I do it in nice straight lines in criss-cross patterns, generally about 50 cuts each go. I've cut up well over 100 times. On occasions I have had to go to casualty and immediately get hauled onto the psychiatric bandwagon. I cut up and if it's deep, I'm sent to casualty. I'm stitched up and inevitably the shrink is called in. I am urged to go into hospital. Sometimes I'm sectioned, so the right to choose has been taken away from me. I am then given a nice little 'label' by the consultant. The current label, incidentally, is Schizophrenia. Then the "treatment" begins. Drugs, of course, and once E.C.T. I am then totally bombed out and regarded as "well again".

The last two weeks have not been untypical. On four occasions in the last fortnight I have been 'strongly' advised to go into hospital. Knowing the system as I do, I have refused point blank. So instead, it's drug treatment - a jab of Depixol in my bum - that'll last a month. They know that I regularly refuse to take mind-altering drugs, hence the jab. At home I have supplies of other 'anti-psychotic' drugs, 'mood stabilisers', Valium and sleepers. I know all their contra-indications. That's why I don't take them. If I did take them I would be standing here like a monosyllabic zombie.

So. That's how the professionals see me. I'm a self-destructive Schizophrenic.

But how do I see myself? First and foremost, I am a survivor of sexual abuse and a survivor of the system. I won't play ball. I know why I self-injure. I do it at times of extreme emotion: anger, self-hatred, stress, grief and guilt. I do it to punish myself. When I feel I am losing control, I reach for a razor and prove to myself that I can, at least, have control over my body.

The cuts are a visual expression of my distress. When I am lost for words, my cuts speak for me. They say - look - **this** is how much I'm hurting inside. So. Is that Schizophrenic? I think not.

When I first cut up I thought I was mad. I didn't know anyone in the world did it. I felt a freak and very isolated. Like Diane, joining the Bristol Crisis Line was a real turning point. Here were other women - bright, lucid and accepting. The majority of them self-injured too. So I was no longer alone. Now I know for a fact that we are not alone. I wrote a magazine article last year on cutting and had over 500 replies from women who thought they were totally isolated and crazy because they self-injured.

There are many ways of self-injuring - cutting up is just one. Anorexia and Bulimia are others. So's alcohol and drug abuse. Not to mention hitting things, burning and scalding oneself, or swallowing non-ingestants like bleach.

I'll tell you what self-injury isn't - and professionals take note. It's not masochistic. It's not attention-seeking. It's rarely a symptom of a so-called psychiatric illness. It's not a suicide attempt. It is not silly and definitely not selfish. I know - because I've been accused of all these things.

So what is it? It's a silent scream. It's about trying to create a sense of order out of chaos. It's a visual manifestation of extreme distress. Those of us who self-injure carry our emotional scars on our bodies.

It can and often does stem from our pre-verbal childhood. When we suffered the trauma of sexual abuse or abandonment. We were left, young and hurt and often angry. But because we couldn't express ourselves, we stayed silent and hid our feelings. Self-hatred inevitably creeps in. Eventually, for many, the only way to deal with terrible childhood experiences and give vent to them is through self-harm.

Women self-harm more than men. As little girls, we are taught to be ladylike and bite our lip. Little boys are encouraged to shout and let off steam. This conditioning inevitably stays with us in adulthood.

But what do we gain from harming ourselves?

Personally, when I've seen the blood run I've felt relieved and purged. The stress recedes and I've felt as though I am back in control of my mind. Once more I have deflected those emotions and painful memories.

Physiologically, when we inflict pain, our body responds by producing Endorphins, our natural opiates or pain relievers that give us a lift and even a temporary feeling of peace.

Now I've told you what the professional's solution to the problem is. But what about what we want? I want a lot of nurturing and the chance to talk, cry, shout and understand. In this respect, my lover, my parents and my friends have been brilliant. They may not understand, but they accept. They don't judge me or criticise me. I also want psychodrama - the chance to get in touch with the child in me and understand it from an adult perspective. A nurse once suggested to me that I could inflict pain on myself without cutting. She'd plonk two ice-cubes in my hands and I had to clasp them until they'd melted. It hurt. But for a while it worked. This day is crucial for all of us. It's a milestone because it's making self-harm a public issue at last. It's easy to lie about scars. Now though, if anyone asks me, I tell them what I do. I don't care if they're strangers, friends or work colleagues. I want to make them aware of the problem and it's enormity, and above all, I want to enlighten them. The normal initial response is shock, but once I've explained about it, they understand, and often feed back their own experiences of self-harm. Dialogue is crucial. I have never lost a friend or colleague through being honest.

Let's take that honesty away with us today and not hide behind our shame. We must destroy the myths and destroy the silence. We must do it for those women, who like us, will turn to self-harm in the future. We must make it easier for them than it has been for us.

Now, it might sound like I'm through with self-harm, having all the insight that I've learned from others and from articles. I'm not. I still cut up. I am still going through the battle. The battle is predominantly with myself, my past, and of course professional ignorance. You rarely come through a battle without scars. I, like many, am battle scarred. But I'm proud. Proud because I am going to win this battle. My scars are my proof.

Thank you for letting me share this with you.

PROFESSIONAL THOUGHT DISORDER PART II:
(This is a round hole - you will be a round peg).

ANDY SMITH

The Role of Major Tranquillisers in Self-Harm.

Major tranquillisers contributed enormously to my need to self-harm. The ability of these "medicines" to limit one's range of expressions to monosyllabic mutterings is astounding. Before taking Major Tranquillisers I had a rich and varied vocabulary. I found the restrictions on my ability to think, in essence a temporary chemical brain damage, so frustrating. The concomitant loss of dignity, bowel and bladder control made the reply I could give to questions such as "How are you feeling?" woefully inadequate. I felt the drugs were rotting me from the inside out. I couldn't tell anyone in words. It wasn't possible to string that many words together. Inside I was screaming. Outside my face was frozen. The occasional foul flatulence being one of the few indications I was still alive. At this stage my intention in self-harming was to communicate the awfulness of my state. I tried to tell the consultant that the so-called symptoms were preferable to this featureless limbo. Each time I was asked to drop my trousers for yet another new hand Hefting the Hypo.. I would refuse, be sent to see the consultant, have it proved to me by some ludicrous analogy that I was off my head and sent back to have the injection. Thus carving the star of David on one arm and an equilateral triangle on the other was, by my usual standards, quite eloquent.

The Role of the Accident & Emergency staff in compounding the effect.

On reflection, the staff attitude, during my many visits to Accident & Emergency, was one of deterrence. This would vary between humiliation and outright physical abuse. The element of humiliation could consist of being told that any discomfort I might be feeling from the festering week old wound in my arm was invalid because there were people there who were injured by accident (I was once slapped round the face for asking if those who had injured themselves by drinking and driving were included). The physical abuse was usually in the form of inadequate anaesthesia to no anaesthesia or analgesics. The one thing that galls me is that I don't believe these people were sadists. I believe they thought they were doing it for my own good. However, I recognise the central part played by this treatment in punishing myself. At the times in my life when I needed my worthlessness confirmed, going to Accident & Emergency with a self-inflicted injury was the perfect way of doing this.

Hiding the evidence.

If my self-harm was attention-seeking, I have to admit to not being very good at it. I would estimate that perhaps only 5 to 10% of my injuries were ever seen by anyone before they had healed and scarred. During my period of most intense self-harm I was living in a Local Authority hostel. The two facts are not unrelated. It was a requirement of residence that one was occupied during the day. I had at this point a rag-bag of qualifications ranging from "C" grade "O" levels to an ability to break and school horses, neither of which impressed the local dole office nor potential employers when coupled with my physical appearance being distorted by the drugs. I was thus forced to work at an Industrial Therapy Unit at a local bin. The unit was called the farm factory as it had once been part of the self sufficiency most Victorian bins had. Now I think it was called this as we had less choice than chickens in a factory farm. My day would start at 6 o'clock as I would try to shake the sleeping pills out of my head, and shake the anti-depressants, tranquillisers and side-effect pills down my throat. I would then catch three buses to get to the bin by 9.30 am. and get a bollocking for being late. The next two and a half hours would be spent performing tasks that wouldn't stretch the intellectual ability of an ant. Lunch would follow on from this. As a vegetarian this would consist of over-cooked cold vegetables and a Kraft cheese slice. A walk round the gardens would lead one back to the farm factory. Another three hours of packing pens. Three buses. Home. Dinner.Evening meeting, where I would then try to justify my existence to an arsehole social worker playing socially dirty tricks. What better way of rounding off the day by slicing your forearm from elbow to wrist?

Being a male self-harmer.

Some of the misconceptions around self-harm includes motivation and perpetrators. My motivations for self-harming were diverse, but included examining the interior of my arms for evidence of hydraulic lines. This may sound strange. But I was sure that being human was not compatible with the degree of difference between you and me. One of us could not be human and as many of you had tried to convince me that you were human then it had to be me. I have tried many times to fit this into a model of attention-seeking. I have yet to succeed. On other occasions my motivation was one of damage limitation. I would be given 'either or' choices by my tormentors. "Either you damage yourself or you damage the person you're angry with". Every time I said "No" the degree of damage I would have to inflict on myself would escalate. The damage was always above the cuff level and below neck level and above ankle level. Attention-seeking? I think not. This range of emotional expression is usually typified as female. I am in no position to say why this is so. I think it has more to do with Psychiatry's need to label and dismiss than with any objective analysis. Further, given my experience and the experiences of others related to me, I fail to understand how any research based on

Accident & Emergency records can ever give anything but a distorted view of the area.

The role of the safety kit in clipping the cycle.

The role of professionals in my ceasing to self-harm is negligible. It was the analysis of why I self-harmed that gave me an answer. As I have mentioned previously, an integral part of the damage was the vilification by the Accident & Emergency staff, so I would carry a safety kit consisting of; a clean sterile blade with which to cut myself, a tube of antiseptic cream, cotton wool, Butterfly steri-strips,plasters and a Crepe bandage. With this I could successfully limit the damage to myself, my self-esteem and my reputation. The effect of this was to lessen the trauma of cutting to the point where I was able to cease.

Louise, you have no insight.
I've been an R.M.N. for 10 years
and I know what normality is.

← (R.M.N. and normal).

Well, if you're a
shining example of
"normality", somebody
pass me a packet
of razor blades.

L.R. Pembroke

MARIE

I find it hard to recall the first time I cut myself, I must have been about 12 or 13 years old. Psychologists and psychiatrists had already labelled me as "out of control". At home I was undergoing so much mental, physical and sexual abuse, I wanted to scream and scream. But I couldn't, I thought it was my fault, something I was doing wrong but I didn't know what.

I saw my brother's razor on the bathroom sink one night and I just thought to myself, if I cut myself, punish myself, I'll be alright. So I cut my wrist. As I watched the blood flow I felt no pain, I just felt clean, released, almost detached from what I had just done. It was like I was screaming without opening my mouth. After that I spent my time in and out of children's homes, foster parents and psychiatric units. I was married for a while with a son, but in secret I was cutting myself and swallowing foreign bodies i.e., batteries, pens, pencils etc. Anything to hurt myself with. One night in desperation after my father's death I set fire to a pile of rubbish in a street. I was sectioned to a Special Hospital. That was four years ago.

I'm still here. 75% of women in Special Hospitals harm themselves one way or another, through cutting, swallowing or inserting. We are labelled as "attention-seeking". No-one really tries to understand why we do it. If we get angry and try to show our feelings then we are labelled, "psychopath", "psychotic", "paranoid", and "personality disordered".

You find you get stitched up without any painkilling injections. No-one takes any interest in why we do these things. **We're just another label and another number.**

HELEN

I began cutting myself at the age of fourteen after numerous years of bullying at school. I was made to feel like a freak and outcast by my peers. It was drummed into me that I was a bad person.

Harming acts as an emotional safety valve. My head often feels like a pressure cooker, I can feel the tension building up and the urge is overwhelming. My feelings just sit there inside of me, waiting to be expressed and I am unable to cry, scream, or get angry. Women are conditioned not to get angry in our society, and the only place left for my anger is to go inwards. I often feel that I am cutting out the **bad** of me. Punishing myself for something. It's a way of coping with life for that moment. My body is just an object which my mind is cut off from.

Self-harmers are often treated with 'kid gloves'. People are often afraid of us. Failing to recognise the emotional side of the problem, focusing on the physical side.

Sometimes I cut myself because I need to **feel something**. At these times I withdraw into myself. At other times, my feelings are so chaotic, vivid and overwhelming, that I have to **cut them out** of me. It's impossible for me to talk or ask for help when the urge to cut is overwhelming.

My self harm comes from a low self esteem, a feeling that everything about me is wrong, and a strong sense of taking responsibility for other people's feelings. It's also a way of expressing and coping with my self hatred albeit temporary.

A sense of 'control' (either in or out of) comes from my self-harm. By overcoming the pain I feel, I have control' over body and thus my life.

I must stress that self-harmers do feel pain to varying degrees and at different times. But the physical pain is far less than the mental pain.

"Attention seeking" or "attempted suicide" are just a couple of the 'professional' myths attached to self-harm. Suicide is final. Self-harm is a release from emotional pain and a struggle for survival.

The whole experience of Accident & Emergency is degrading for self-harmers. It just perpetuates the vicious circle. I am made to feel that I'm wasting their time and resources which results in me hating myself even more. This sustains my cutting. If only Accident & Emergency staff could realise that it would be easier for them and us if they treated us humanely. I have had some supportive responses from Accident & Emergency staff. Such as when they haven't criticised or judged me for what I do, and have been prepared to listen and treat me just like any other patient.

My first admission to a psychiatric hospital was quite a shock for me. I felt that I was expected to conform to an image of "appropriate behaviour" as defined by the staff. I found it impossible to express any kind of emotion just in case it was misinterpreted or labelled. When I did show signs of distress their answer to my pain was Major Tranquillisers. I was not encouraged to talk about my feelings and express my emotions, and the tranquillisers left me feeling numb as my self-harm does. I felt as though my identity had been stripped from me and that childlike passivity was the role I was expected to adopt. On one occasion, I burnt myself and failed to get any medical treatment from the staff. They obviously perceived my actions as "attention seeking". I felt as if they'd washed their hands of me. It was stressed that this was, *"a psychiatric hospital, not a general one"*. My physical needs were ignored to the same extent as my emotional needs.

I became concerned about being Sectioned and was told that I *"couldn't be sectioned"* as I didn't have a "mental illness". That if I did, I would have a *"Personality Disorder"*. This quite clearly shows the needs of psychiatrists to label and stereotype patients according to textbook definitions rather than seeing them as individuals. I was also told that I was *"not a danger to myself"*. It all depends on what you define as being a "danger to self"! In my eyes it was clear that I was. It was obvious that they didn't take me or my self-harm seriously.

My family's reaction to my self-harm was one of anger and bewilderment. They believed that I was trying to hurt them. After a number of family therapy sessions they realised that I wasn't trying to hurt them but punish myself. My family tried to stop me from hurting myself but it was useless as they couldn't hide everything sharp away from me.

Before I can stop self-harming I need to feel self-worth and become assertive. I need to learn how to stand up for the rights I am so frequently denied. To gain confidence, self-respect and esteem.

The best way to help self-harmers is to listen, allow them to express their feelings, and allow them to feel in control and **believe** in them. The most helpful thing for me has been talking to others in similar situations. They accept me as I am **with** or **without** my self-harm. They give me **hope.**

PROFESSIONAL THOUGHT DISORDER PART VI:
(Respecting a persons distress)

ROSALIND CAPLIN

Overt self-harm did not come easy to me - although I had been subtly abusing my body since I was 14 - direct, self-inflicted mutilation was an anathema. My first few psychiatric admissions brought me into daily contact with those others whose scarred and wounded flesh so mirrored my own deep inner distress - that I would have to turn away in horror..sick..

It was a year later when I first drew the razor blades over my wrist. The memory is poignant to me even 23 years later. At 16, a psychiatric inmate for virtually the past 2 years, I was a social, emotional and spiritual wreck. I wandered the ward, a ghostlike figure, shadow of the self I was trying so desperately to find and connect with. Introverted, dazed and abused by forced feeding and vast cocktails of tranquillisers, anti-depressants and sleeping pills, life had no meaning, no reality - no hope - even my dreams, all I had to live for, had been brutally shattered at my feet, I was imprisoned in a cage where no-one could reach me; even myself.

Then one evening the inner pain, the deep aching became so strong that I felt it was burning a hole right through my body. It became so unbearable - so, so agonising that for the first time I really wanted to die. I locked myself in the bathroom and slowly started to scrape - feeling my inner pain surfacing as the blood began to ooze through my skin. But it felt all too much. In tears I went and showed the staff my distress, all I so longed for was to be heard, acknowledged, cared for and loved. Instead I received more medication and a course of 15 E.C.T.'s. Fine substitute to emotional distress.

It was six months before I again self-harmed. I was a four and a half stone labelled 'anorexic' - under a year's section in a notorious asylum. I was kept in virtual isolation for the first three months - my cell-like room measuring about 6ft x 6ft. The only window was so high up that I could not even reach it by standing on the bed - so I saw no outside world, only the hazy trauma of ward activities and personal and others' distresses.

For those months all my activities, eating, sleeping, using the bedpan and washing were contained within its confines. If I ventured out I would be dragged back and thrown onto the bed by a member of staff.

I dreaded the days as I hated the nights - living in constant fear for my sanity - for my survival. Each mealtime would herald a series of physical abuses as I was held down, food being shoved irreverently down my screaming throat. I would be left bruised, battered with scratches all round my mouth and face - exhausted, bloated and in severe physical pain and mental anguish. My body was no longer mine, they had violated it - they had taken it over and were trampling all over it - my psyche was forced to retreat - that was the only way I could have survived.

They called it behavioural therapy - a system, somewhat arbitrary, of rewards and punishments, depending upon how 'good' and compliant one was. I knew if I played their game, ate my food, did what they wanted and gave them an easier time I would likewise be better treated and sooner discharged. However even through my distress I realised that at all costs - I **HAD** to remain true to myself - and I knew that cost to be severe.

I felt more and more like a caged animal - crazily walking my room looking for escape - waiting in sultry hope day in day out for some ray of sunshine - for some awakening from this nightmare. But there was none. I lived in a state of fear - constantly being on guard against attack - lost and alone in a frightening and alien world. And no-one saw my distress. No-one could relate it to the layers of abuse that every day were inflicted upon me - to the promised 'rewards' such as going to the lavatory or having a bath alone..or even being 'allowed' to dress - that never materialised. No, to them I was a spoilt little girl 'acting out' in order to gain the attention of others..My perversity at refusing to eat such vast amounts of hospitalised food required punishing..if I so blatantly refused to help myself 'get better' - then they would have to force me..

I became increasingly threatened and angry by this punitive regime. The anger grew and grew within me until it seemed my whole body would split unless it came out - so I began to smash plates and bang my head against the walls until I felt dizzy and sick. These last attempts to try and make them see, to make them try and understand - were seen as a call to increase my Chlorpromazine to 600 mg a day and restrict any so-called privileges I may have 'earned' through having gained weight..

So what else could I do - I was forced into the position of withdrawal, of silence..just as they forced food and medication down my throat, so they also forced down my anger. So I began cutting my wrists and arms because that was the only way to get that rage out of my body. The food somehow stayed down - the medications had their own psychological effects, yet my rage was like that of a tiger being stalked in the jungle - it was alive, moving, both frightened and frightening - an all consuming fire that grew and grew inside me until I could no longer live with it - it had to come out or my body would not survive its ferocity.

And each scraping of physical flesh, the pain, the blood, the mortal sacrifice was as much an acknowledgement of survival -of Life - as it was a ritualistic act of revenge. Except it was directed against myself.

Years of superficial abuse followed until only recently, perhaps the last 6 months, when I realised on a deeper level for the first time the impact that years of eating distress and self-harm had had on my body - and I began to feel so sad - sad because those experiences were something I had to endure, sad because of all the many consequences of such psychiatric and self-abuse, many that were not reversible. But more so because I now realised that in spite of everything I did want to live, and I wanted to live while my physical body still had strength and health enough within it.

I still feel the serpent poison, I still get those unbearable urges when my body feels 'taken over' - possessed as it were by an entity far larger than myself. I feel myself bloat out as I feel the scream rising. But I am beginning to make links between inner and outer reality - to ask this feeling what it is about - to try in whatever way I possibly can to divert the impulse, because I know, ultimately, for me, that is not what it is. I am angry, angry, angry yes - I am starting, tentatively perhaps, to own it, to see it as having a positive creativity, passion and clarity of vision. It need not be self-destructive and all-consuming but contains within it also my will to live.

LOUISE ROXANNE PEMBROKE

I do not view any expression of distress as pathological or intrinsically as a psychiatric phenomenon. People labelled as being "mentally ill" experience and express feelings/perceptions which people usually deny or dismiss. It is possible for all of us to experience **'perceptual differences'**. To become aware of things that are not usually seen or heard. To develop dialogue with different entities from different dimensions of reality. It's just that some of us either willingly or unwillingly acknowledge and listen to them. They are **not** "*hallucinations*" or "*delusions*". Hallucinations are usually caused by serious physical illness, trauma or drugs and are qualitatively and quantitatively different. I have hallucinated during physical illness and the difference between that and my contact with my spirits and voices are very clear to me. It is not possible to have a dialogue with a hallucination that is organic in cause and temporary. It is possible to communicate with perceptual differences. They are real and have meaning, origin and history. There is a lot to learn from them, and we should be interacting with them as opposed to trying to obliterate them with tranquillisers. Sometimes, these differences can be metaphors or an external form for intolerable feelings to talk back to us. The common shared concept of reality can be overwhelming, and other realities develop which can be both life-threatening and life-enriching. These realities are not meaningless and can be understood.

At 10 years of age new and different perceptions awoke in and around me. I became aware of other human spirits, one of which I had contact with for 7 years. I also became aware of sexism, racism and other global oppressions. I could see my pre-ordained role as a white girl. That a girl's worth was gauged by her appearance; that expressions of anger and assertion were not easily tolerated; that my low place in society's pecking order had nothing to do with me as an individual but connected to the maintenance of a hierarchy of white male dominance.

At 17 years of age I reached an apocalyptic crisis. I was a student at a leading dance school, seriously eating distressed and with a collapsing sense of self-worth. When I became aware of my **own** spirit leaving my body for the first time I was devastated. I assumed that my spirit had died and I attempted suicide by overdose. I was found by the police and taken to Accident and Emergency in a distressed state. This was my first contact with hospital services.

I could not talk, and I couldn't understand why I had not fallen asleep and died. My overwhelming fear on arrival was- what is going to happen? I was undressed, put on a trolley and the nurse looked through my bag. On finding a dance studio membership card she announced, "Oh an actress, what would you expect?". She then informed me that I would be given a "Gastric-Lavage". I did not understand what this was and was too distressed to ask, so I cried even more. Her response to my cries of fear of the unknown was, "Well you shouldn't have done it should you?". Several pairs of hands pinned me to the trolley whilst the treatment was carried out. When they had finished they walked away and I was left alone for quite a while, so I tried to leave thinking that was it. I wandered onto a ward and was put to bed. As the doctor took blood I screamed because I couldn't speak. I couldn't say, "I'm frightened, what is happening?". My scream was silenced by a nurse sitting on my chest whilst the doctor finished taking the blood sample. The next morning I was transferred to a medical ward where the nursing and medical staff were kind and approachable. However, my first experience of Accident & Emergency had left me feeling that I must be a bad person who was going to be punished. I didn't talk about how I felt, I just said as little as possible and only when requested to speak. I went home on Friday and returned to dance school on Monday. I could not tell anyone how I felt.

A few months later I was admitted to a ward on the eating disorder unit known as "The Dorm". This admission was to become the catalyst for my self-harm. Starting my tour of the psychiatric services I soon realised just how narrow the acceptable range of expression of distress is. I had to learn not to express anger and frustration towards what felt like torture. I could not express my pain and anger to the people who were controlling every aspect of my life. I had to learn to scream silently.

During my psychiatrisation I tried hard to behave in the way that was expected of me. Trying to achieve the illusive "Appropriate Behaviour" but to no avail. I failed miserably at being a 'good' patient. Something was very wrong with the treatment but I didn't have the language or analysis to articulate it beyond refusing to co-operate with it. I was one of six young women and one man who were subject to Behaviour Modification. Behaviour *Manipulation* is perhaps a more accurate description. My experience of this regime was of ceremonial degradation. The psychological damage it wreaked has long outlived even the pain of forced drugging. Punishment and Reward programmes are merely brain-washing. Punitive tortures that leave people with no outlet for their distress or explosive emotion. It was treating distress as merely aberrant behaviour. Preventing people from doing something by conditioning with a carrot and stick, force-feeding or force-dieting people into an image of perceived 'normality' may only relieve the observers concern. Peer pressure is an immensely powerful tool. It was also used in concentration camps.

Everybody had to stay at the table until all had finished, otherwise all were punished in the face of dissent. We were pushed into punishing each other. It felt like being a Jew having to push your friends into the gas chamber to save your own skin. For six hours a day we would sit at the table eating and drinking. The length of time was prolonged due to underweight individuals being in great physical pain through being fed enormous amounts of food that made no medical or humane sense. It felt like dietary rape. People would start to invent games that nobody could win. Chips would be cut into two, then four, then six. Psychiatry can make you do strange things in order to deal with their treatment. These would start *after* admission. We were confined to the dormitory where we would eat, sleep and defecate into bedpans. 'Privileges' had to be 'earned' through 'good' behaviour. Privileges included access to the toilets and leaving the dormitory. 'Good' behaviour meant doing exactly as you were told and agreeing with the staff's interpretation of your life and problems. Disagreement was viewed as a symptom of your "illness", or being just plain difficult. Rebellion took many forms. One woman was deaf, had 'tunnel vision' and could not sign or lip-read. All communication had to be in writing. In the weekly ward meetings with the junior doctors she would be ignored. They made little or no attempt to include her in the conversation, whilst the rest of us talked about food because that was the expectation. Throwing her plates of food was the only way her scream would be heard. One evening, she refused to drink her *Complan* and like caged animals we turned on ourselves. Her dissent would have resulted in punishment for all, so she was held to her chair by her fellow inmates and attempts were made to force the *Complan* down her throat. Whilst this was happening the nurse observing us sat impassively and watched. The woman was dragged off to the locked dormitory for the night.

It was around this time that I started to self-harm. I did not 'learn' it, as I was not aware that anybody else engaged in it. It was the only way to cope with and express the pain I felt. There seemed to be no other outlet.

The similarities with caged animals struck me as I watched a programme on vivisection. One experiment provided a parallel with my experience of psychiatry. In the experiment a monkey was restrained and put in a cage. Its anger was supposedly going to be controlled through punishment via electric shocks. The monkey initially bit furiously at the surrounding cage. After numerous shocks it started to bite **itself**. The behaviourist approach does this to people too.

There were many arguments and much confusion in the dorm. Some women felt that their physical health didn't matter as long as they didn't look thin or ill. Others felt that they were only taken 'seriously' when drastically physically ill. Some became institutionalised going back every few months for years. Others would 'normalise', forcing themselves to fit into other peoples' criteria of what was viewed as 'normal' and healthy at great cost. Sexist and heterosexist attitudes were common amongst the staff. The oppression and discrimination that I was aware of in the world around me were mirrored within the psychiatric services, actively practised and reinforced.

Care with make-up and hairstyle was seen to be clear indications of 'getting better'. Likewise wanting marriage and children were viewed by some as part of recovery. Individuals have been told that their problems would get better if they simply acquired a boyfriend. Gender issues were never discussed in a political context.

I witnessed a greater propensity for sexual taunting and voyeurism of those of us labelled as 'eating disordered' by one male nurse. This abuse was presented as part of the 'treatment'. He felt that he could harass or tease women by claiming to be testing out our 'recovery' from our alleged problems of hating female bodily contours and being sexually repressed. Cure and eradication of the aberrant behaviour were the goals. It felt as if my soul would be the price. On leaving hospital I came to the devastating realisation that I could not fit in outside nor be what the so-called experts wanted of me. I could not be a 'normal' person or a 'good' patient. On returning home I knew that my dancing career was over. I was never going to return to school and fulfil my life's ambition of becoming a choreographer and form my own dance company. I spent the next two years going through psychiatric and Accident and Emergency services.

I tried hard to convince myself that my perceptions were not real, but it didn't work. I became more distressed by denying what I felt. By giving up ownership of my experiences and the right to self-determination I was allowing my self-respect to be stolen from me. Ownership had gone to the blue file in the filing cabinet. It took a long time before I could regain ownership.

I was aware of the iatrogenic helplessness and dependency of my fellow patients, and I knew that I did not want to become yet another shuffling passive recipient. All aspects of my life were categorised in pigeon-holes that prevented me from knowing how things related. My entire life was reduced to a list of symptoms and ridiculed with labels that took the meaning from my distress. I became aware that people deemed "chronic" had become so because of the process of dehumanisation, misunderstanding and inappropriate responses. People stay voluntarily incarcerated in the system. If you are identified as a leper - then obviously you must go to the leper colony, where you will at least be accepted on the basis of being a leper. When you go to hospital you are told what is wrong with you, and what the solution is to your particular category. You continually return, there is nothing else. Psychiatric services keep people dependent and helpless through many different processes including, "Expertise", "Professionalism", chemicals and threat.

Initially I kept my self-harm secret. When talking to a fellow patient I discovered that I was not alone. It was only when the injuries became too difficult for me to conceal that I approached a member of staff. My fellow patient warned me that the staff would not tolerate self-harm. She said they would 'wash their hands of me' - a very accurate prediction. During that admission nurse informed me I would be jeopardising my chances of receiving psychotherapy, as "therapists did not take cutters". I felt I was on everybody's scrap heap. I felt condemned. The response from the psychiatric hospital ranged from anger with punishment to indifference. Occasionally I was stitched with no anaesthetic, I suppose to teach me a lesson. I would dread telling the staff, some were openly angry and hostile. On one occasion waiting in the clinic room for the doctor to arrive nursing staff abused me, with remarks like; "you're wasting the doctor's time". No one wanted to talk about it beyond "why did you do it?". I could not find the words to describe, cutting had become the language to describe the pain, communicating everything I felt. It was viewed as silly and attention-seeking. For me it was the only way I could survive. The various labels don't help. Calling me "neurotic", transforms the act of self-harm to "attention-seeking". While "psychotic" changes self-harm to "understandable".

On being diagnosed as suffering from the "1st rank symptoms of Schizophrenia" and "catatonia", neuroleptic drugs were now on the menu. After being discharged from a Section of the Mental Health Act I attended the day hospital and reluctantly took depot injections. The penny finally dropped when a fellow patient told me about the effects of the drugs (side-effects is a euphemism). Information that I had asked for and been denied. I decided to get away from psychiatry's control, to stay meant my life was at risk. My social worker attempted to place me at a social service day centre. I was rejected on the grounds that I was too much of a danger to myself. I tried to get support from a counselling service, but was refused and told to return to my consultant. Years later I found out that the consultant had instructed both the day centre and the counselling service to turn me away in an attempt to make me go back to him. I was told that I looked so much "better" whilst taking neuroleptic drugs but the reality was different for me. In fact their effects, such as emotional blunting merely made self-harming easier - as pain and fear are dulled.

One psychiatrist silenced an attempt to discuss self-harm with "only you can stop doing that. I can't help you". I was perfectly aware of this, but I needed to talk about it. My doctor only wanted to record how many times I had attended Accident and Emergency since my last appointment.

I became well known to the local Accident and Emergency department. For over two years I visited it at least monthly, sometimes twice a week. I was insulted, condemned, even ridiculed. It takes days to recover from that trauma. They assumed that the problem was being addressed by the psychiatrist while he was treating me. They did not realise nobody wanted to talk about it. I did not tell anyone about what was happening to me in Accident and Emergency. I became so used to being treated as worthless, I let them do and say what ever they wanted. I internalised **their** degradation. Some Accident and Emergency staff treated me badly because they knew they could. I might as well have a neon sign over my head saying 'kick my head in'. One casualty officer always instructed whoever was going to stitch me to not bother with sewing each layer of tissue separately. Just a skin suture was to be used. Each time my injury became infected. I felt unable to say anything. My injuries became increasingly serious, my G.P. warned me about the risk of permanent damage. At the time this information didn't penetrate.

I tried to keep away from psychiatric services. This was extended to the Accident and Emergency department, going to Accident and Emergency had become a form of self-harm. The judgement of the staff, confirmed that I really was the lowest form of life and reinforced every negative feeling I had ever had about myself. I could no longer stomach Accident and Emergency so I stopped. At first I didn't know how to look after myself and finished up with many infections, including septicaemia. When I became friends with an ophthalmic nurse, a turning point was reached. Ostensibly she treated me for an eye condition, I took a risk and showed her a serious injury. I was adamant I would not go to hospital. She agreed to help me, and in a non-judgmental atmosphere I first saw the practical care I really needed. I started to carry a clean blade and a first-aid kit around with me. This was liberating and I harmed myself less. I had cut out one part of the cycle of degradation - Accident and Emergency. I did this for five years and for two years I managed not to self-harm, during which time I had cosmetic surgery to my scars.

As I emerged from the darkness of psychiatry I had a sense of great injustice and was very angry. I met other people who had similar experiences in survivor groups. It felt safe to talk about the debasement and disempowerment I felt in hospital. A sense of liberation and empowerment came through the release and recognition of anger. I learned I did not need a medical framework to define myself and my experience. I regained ownership of my self and my distress. I stopped pursuing the twin gods of 'cure' and 'normality'. I encompassed my distress, trying to learn from it. I started to find ways of limiting the damage. I discovered that by self-harming as soon as I had the urge, I would sustain less damage than if I held out against it for several days. Everytime I managed to redirect that energy in a non-harming way it was celebrated by my peers. A partner in a relationship encouraged me to smash crockery to ease mounting tension. Having permission and space to externalise pain and anger is a powerful option. I gradually became involved with the user/survivor/self-advocacy movement and made the transition from disempowered to empowered with a strong commitment to work with others for change and alternatives to conventional dogmatic services. This movement is fighting in the same way that blacks and gays do. This is no weird concept of 'consumerism' but a **social** and **political** struggle. The movement is doing important work for **all** of society, not just psychiatric survivors. With help from my peers, I became a campaigner and trainer. Working with survivor groups and professionals here and abroad. I also worked in the statutory and voluntary sectors of care provision.

At a stressful time in my life, my self-injury became serious again. I could not continue to look after my injuries. After an allergic reaction to 'steri-strips' I was forced to go to Accident and Emergency again. I found it increasingly difficult to deal with my injuries and needed someone else to do the practical part. Going back to Accident and Emergency was hard as an ex-mental health worker. It equalled failure, and I felt as though I was giving up responsibility for my injuries. The severity and my inability to look after myself left me with no other option.

The pattern and process of my self-harm changed considerably and I became increasingly isolated by my perceptual differences. The external voices, mutation of my body, and attacks by animal spirits have made work impossible, and contact with other people extremely difficult. My own spirit left my body with increasing frequency. She would not return to my body until she had evidence that I was alive and human. The only proof I could give her was to cut into my body. This is the only confirmation she will accept. She has to see inside my body in order to return. I needed to cut more often to retrieve my spirit. All the time she is out of my body I can hear her scream. She is held by a still unknown force. I feel the pain of her torture. I need to self-harm in order to keep alive. I have had to develop new ways to try to limit the damage. This has evolved to cutting very slowly, at times over 2-3 hours. Enabling me to see where I am cutting in order to avoid major blood vessels and tendons. If I cut myself quickly, I know from past experience that it can result in an injury to the bone with the attendant serious risks. This degree of damage limitation is exercising 'control' through cycles of self-harm that needed treatment 3-4 times a week. Although the frequency leaves me feeling 'out of control'. Self-harm can be both 'in control' and 'out of control' simultaneously. The start of a cycle is often sudden, sometimes on waking up in the morning. There is no time to do anything to prevent it. After the initial injury the urge to self-harm is powerful and constant. It feels like an electrical current running through my body. An intense, unseen war in myself where there is no winning move. I

need to cut my body but I don't **want** to. As my spirits' demands increase, I harm other parts of my body but it is never sufficient. Attacks from my perceptual differences make communications difficult. I am not able to be with friends or family much, the casualty officer is sometimes the first person I've seen all week. Going to hospital after harming myself, waiting to be seen I feel terrified about the way I will be treated. By the time the doctor sees me I just want to blend into the walls. Each time I am treated with disgust or annoyance the cycle is prolonged. It really makes a difference if I am treated with dignity and respect. At the very least it makes the walk home easier. Someone 'caring' for me helps me to punish myself less because of the self-harm.

I have tried lots of ways to limit my self harm. Once I asked for my arms to be plaster-casted for a couple of weeks. I felt so desperate to stop cutting. No doctor was prepared to discuss it with me, my desperation reached an intolerable pitch. I overdosed to stop me from cutting. My own actions left me feeling degraded and the treatment for the overdose added to that degradation. I feared the consequences of telling them why I needed to cut, so I didn't tell them. This resulted in a hazy diagnosis with a prognosis of "incurable" (all in 15 minutes). The medical houseman was often abusive during my stay. He informed me my liver might fail and that a liver transplant would be necessary. He said this as if reading from a list, without looking at me and left as soon as he finished. It is hard to imagine a patient being told that they might have cancer and need chemotherapy without any concern for their feelings. Nor waiting to see whether any questions need answering. By the time I was discharged I felt it may have been better if I had died. I believe that everyone has the **right** to give up, but **no one** has the right to write off another's life.

A few months later I was Sectioned, the reasons were unclear but I was aware they did not include my self-harm. During this admission I experienced bizarre contradictions. At first my belongings were removed from me and I was closely observed. I was allowed out for 2 hours a day. If I returned home for a day, I was body searched for blades on my return. However, on my 2 hours leave each day I could return without being searched. A chemist shop lay handily across the road from the hospital! Logic has never been psychiatry's strongest point. Addressing my self-injury was quickly dropped, I was told nothing could be done about it. Whilst attempting to contain it for myself I smashed a cup to release mounting tension. I do not view this as unacceptable and had no intention of harming myself or anyone else. The responses to my actions culminated in violence. It was made clear that I had to take the medication orally, otherwise I would be forcibly injected. The dose given was higher than the prescribed dose. A couple of hours later I was forced to take another equally high dose. By the time the night staff came on duty I was lying on my bed unable to move, utterly sedated. The night nurse lifted my head and rammed the medicine cup in to my mouth. I wondered why they did this? I could hardly run away. All that for a smashed cup when a hug would have been infinitely more beneficial. I later explained to my 'key' nurse why I had done it and she assured me that I would not be drugged into oblivion if I did it again.

A few months later my distress again led to suicide. As it seemed that it was the only positive decision I could take. My spirit was not returning to my body when I self-harmed. I realised that no amount of harm would return her to me. I could not continue without her. Body and soul can not survive independently. Consequently my body must be destroyed for my spirit to survive. Although she would not return, the drive to cut myself continued. My perceptual differences kept me house-bound and isolated. I had a poor quality of life. Being unable to do anything useful or productive left me with no sense of self-value.

I felt angry at my failure to kill my self. I spent many weeks eating and vomiting until I was too exhausted to be angry.

I realised that there were times when I needed to be kept 'safe' and be out of the environment of where I harmed myself or had easy access to blades. In the next cycle of self-harm I took the extreme risk of asking for an admission. This went against my beliefs about psychiatry and is a measure of the depth of my desire not to harm. A psychiatric ward was the last place I wanted to be, my desire to not be stitched for the fourth consecutive night was even greater. Psychiatry has the monopoly on resources. Leaving little resource or space for non-medical crisis facilities. With the support of my friend I went to Accident and Emergency before I injured again. What I was looking for was help for a few days to keep myself safe and away from razor blades. Until the drive to cut and my perceptual differences had lessened to a copeable degree. I was admitted and the staff showed some understanding of my needs. However, refusal of medication was viewed as *"refusal of treatment"*. I felt under covert pressure to be taking the medication. I was told the refusal would lengthen my stay in hospital. And if I really wanted to get better I should take it. I knew that there would be no point in taking drugs that impair my ability to fight the onslaught of external voices and animal spirits. My insecurity was heightened when I was subject to sexual harassment by another patient, the staff response was ineffectual. One male nurse told the man; *"Don't harass Louise, she's a respectable woman"*. What about harassment of women not viewed as "respectable"? What constituted "respectability"? Asylum was impossible so I discharged myself having decided that my safety might be at greater risk by remaining. I felt deflated and sad: I had been prepared to put aside my negative feelings about services. I wanted to negotiate a plan of action that might have enabled me to contain my self-harm.

I never returned to that hospital's Accident and Emergency department after I was told by a doctor that my injuries were not worth treating anymore because they where self-inflicted.

Going to another Accident and Emergency department I asked if they treated self-inflicted injuries. The nurse appeared shocked that I should ask such a question. She assured me there would be no discrimination. I still do not feel sure about my right to treatment. One doctor has stated he felt that there may be a point in refusing treatment whilst I continued refusing to see a psychiatrist. A psychiatrist reinforced the threat. Telling me if I did not find 'alternatives', the casualty staff would 'see no point' in treating my injuries. Other staff have not taken this stance. One particular doctor has been helpful. His sense of outrage at the previous refusal of treatment meant that I felt my pain acknowledged. He has treated me at all times with dignity and respect. He has never treated me as a 'no-hoper'. His attitude means that whenever I am treated by him I have walked away feeling less anxious and self-punishing than usual. On one occasion he told me that he **respected** me - I almost fell out of the chair in shock. My last cycle of self-harm changed. I removed skin completely and required a skin-graft. My skin appeared 'alien' to me, and felt as if something was crawling underneath it. The only way I could relieve the alienation was by tearing it out with my teeth and a blade. Simultaneously I was under intense attacks from the voices and spirits compounded by sleep deprivation. This culminated in a Section 2.

On reflection, I can see that I needed to be detained for the protection of my skin-graft. I would however, have recovered much quicker if I had remained on the general ward for a few days as opposed to being transferred to a psychiatric hospital. General trained nurses have a greater ability than their psychiatric counter-parts to have 'ordinary' conversations with people. They don't make it feel like a psychiatric check-list of symptoms each time. In my experience, they also find it easier to give basic human comfort. An example of positive intervention was provided by the nurse accompanying me to the psychiatric hospital. As I was being physically attacked by animal spirits I struggled to cover both my ears as the spirits threatened to force their way in. One of my arms was still painful from the surgery so I grasped the nurse's hand to that ear which she duly kept covered. This was helpful.

I absconded from the ward but not very efficiently. I left without putting my contact lens in. I walked several miles in the opposite direction to my home getting lost in the process. I had been carrying the lens in my bag but I just did not think to put it in. My friend pointed out that my inability to do the basics were probably an indication that I was not together enough to be at home, a police van returned me to the hospital.

When I returned, I explained to the nurse what support I felt I needed and could accept as I had done the year before. Clearly, the concept of *damage limitation* was difficult for the nurse to accept. She had the mistaken idea that after a spell in hospital I would *never* harm myself again.

The danger of course would be when I was back at home with easy access to blades, so I tried to explain the idea of early, short-term safe-keeping in an acute cycle of self-harm. That my objective would be to attempt to 'catch' it earlier and earlier thus limiting further or more serious damage. Thus limiting the damage caused by going to the Accident and Emergency departments. This was to "buy time" whilst finding a way to stop. One response to this proposal was,"Don't you want to get married have children?" We were working at cross purposes. Their priorities are Diagnosis and Treatment. The crunch point came when they began to impose "Behaviour Modification". I decided that no-one was going to do that to me again as I knew how damaging it would be, so I arranged to be taken away from the hospital to a safe place. This time I put my contact lens in and went in the right direction. At the next ward round I was discharged in my absence because it was clear to them that I would *"never work with them"*.

There are lessons to be learnt from the above "breakdowns" in help. I know that it is easy for me to be shouldered with all the blame for being incapable of accepting help. I am defenceless against this accusation. Responding to people who self-harm is not easy. I know that some people have genuinely felt an impulse to help and have felt frustrated or confused by the outcome. Others have shown no insight or compassion for what it is like being me. I am not easy to assist and I find it hard to trust others' attempts but some basic ground rules are clear. The most important is that I am listened to, that I am not invaded by the judgement of others or simplistic solutions. (eg, "Just stop doing it") I am able to accept assistance, but on the basis of the helper/s building an alliance and respecting my knowledge of my needs, acting on that information rather than theories that they have been taught.

I am lucky to have friends and family who have stood by me, and accept me however I am. I don't know when, how or if I might stop needing to self-harm. Unless I can find spiritual peace I know I will continue to need treatment for my injuries. Ideally I need access to survivor-led/run non-medical services. I am not alone in wanting that and those of us who live with self-harm have got to fight for these alternatives. Too many people need them. We must make it a reality.

Expertise, Professionalism and Personal power.

Three powerful concepts.

The professional is there as an "expert" to find a way of solving or curing the distress. The recipient receives. There is no understanding on a subjective basis. There is no acceptance of the individual's reality. No common language. I had to search hard to find my own words - as I had become saturated with the language of labels and categories. The language of objectification and mentalism. One aspect of mentalism is the process of not allowing people to express themselves. Psychiatry's range of descriptions of our distress is couched solely in negative terms. A persons behaviour is never labelled in a positive way. "Illness" equals unwanted, bad, abnormal. Something that should be eradicated or cured. However "normal" is not defined, so how can abnormal be determined? Can anyone tell me when the whole population were tested and how to determine, for example, the normal amount of grief to express on the death of your mother? I have heard people say that "mental health" is the absence of "mental illness". About as logical as saying that happiness is the absence of sadness or life is the absence of death. This is not logical. Sadly our society takes seriously the unquantified, flimsy notions of mental health/mental illness, and diagnostic labels. These terms devalue and demean people fundamentally. This devaluation is hard to lose.

Once past the 'relief response' on learning a name for the distress - the label itself does not alleviate the pain. It does not help the professional or the individual to understand what is happening or what would assist the individual. It stops the individual from **owning** the experience and finding his/her **own** language and interpretation. Disempowerment of this kind drives people crazy. It causes people to **be** and **stay** "mentally ill". I don't condemn people accepting their labels - the acceptance is often borne out of desperation. I feel sad that this acceptance can prevent an individual discovering their own description. Along with the labels comes myth and stereotypes perpetuated by the services and continued by society. For example; so-called *"schizophrenics"* are supposed to not be able to make a decision. So-called *"Personality Disordered"* are not meant to be able to hold "normal" social relationships. These mean that the labelled people are seen as inferior or less competent. In the same way that stereotypes of Afro-Caribbean and Asian people equal inferiority. It is common amongst those who have used or been used by the services to feel that they are not able to be responsible because they are incompetent and inadequate. Low self-esteem and confidence foster these feelings. If people are treated in a certain way, as an 'inadequate', then invariably they will respond as an 'inadequate' person. People become dependant and helpless with the treatments and labels. They are crushed if given options not choice and identity is defined by psychiatry's labels. The emphasise is on what the person **can't do**, not what the person **can do**. People often submit themselves to the services for a long time because there is little else - it is clung to - even if hated. Eventually you don't recognise the oppression.

I have come to the conclusion that **people** are not studied by psychiatry and psychology merely categorised and described. That their rigid frameworks serve only to fragment people, turning a break-up into a breakdown. In categorising the distress the distress itself is not acknowledged. The individuals right to **own** the experience has been stolen.

Psychiatric training disables the workers' ability to perceive. The medical and nursing disciplines are taught to see certain sets of images. Every person is compared to the learnt set. Different images and interpretations are not seen. This process leads to treating people as a falsely homogenous group. It is unhelpful and damaging to group together people's distress.

Self-Harm and its Psychiatric Interpretation.

A friend, Diane, rang the Royal College of Psychiatrists and asked for information about services for self-harm and the relevant literature. "Um-er" was the illuminating response. There is confusion over what self-harm is and there is no available information about any services. The only recommended literature is a book on attempted suicide. This just about sums up their disinterest in the subject.

Last year I read about an "ambitious" study being undertaken at Ashworth Special Hospital to look into why so many female patients self-harm. They found, *"The behaviour often represented an attempt to wrest a degree of control from an over-whelming controlling environment"*. Does this really require a degree in psychology to work out? What really galls me is the quote that the staff felt that *"any response appears to reinforce the behaviour"*. The telling statement from the women patients was that they wanted to be with *"people who care"*. They had suggestions, such as being in less secure settings and being offered therapies such as anger management. Did anyone listen to their suggestions? Having visited Ashworth I can understand how even the environment contributed to the need to self-harm. The woman I visited self-harmed and she wanted to start a support group on her ward, but was told that it was too *"risky"*.

In the book, "Bodies under siege - Self Mutilation in Culture and Psychiatry" by Armando R.Favazza. M.D. with Barbara Favazza.M.D. Some of the treatment anecdotes defy belief. A treatment plan was devised where the patient was hospitalised for six weeks. During which time the patient had to agree to no privacy. To be put under "close observation" or "specialling" 24 hours a day. Medication and the **wearing of leather gloves** by the patient were available. The leather gloves made my jaw drop but the following left me speechless, *"Impressed by the ritualistic nature of her cutting, I decided upon a behavioural approach reportedly successful with obsessive-compulsive patients. My plan was to have Janet fantasise about a typical cutting episode. Then, just as she was about to cut herself, I would attempt to stop the fantasy by blowing a whistle and shouting, "Stop! You will not cut yourself! You are in control!"*

This doctor further encouraged "Janet" to fantasise about cutting, substituting a large eraser for a razor. During the whistle and shouts he poured a glass of cold water over her head. Unsurprisingly, his 'therapy' didn't work as "Janet" became seriously eating distressed.

Also the book describes a "pragmatic measure";

"Conducted within the context of a positive relationship that includes concern and caring for the suffering patient, the measure consists of a challenging interpretation of a self-mutilative symptom, given with the express intention of arousing such an emotional response as will counteract the symptom. This can be achieved by an interpretation that attaches unacceptable ideas and emotions to the target symptom. Sexual challenging interpretations are especially effective; for example, "I am afraid that your skin cutting is a perverted form of masturbation". When the patient angrily attacks the interpretation as untrue, the therapist does not argue but rather comments, "The interpretation must be valid because otherwise you would not be so angry about it".

Can you imagine the effect that this might have on an individual who had been sexually abused? As for being offensive in an attempt to make the individual feel so bad that she/he would stop self-harming is a pointless exercise. We are already used to doctors being offensive to us. If I were in the patient's position in the above "sexual challenging interpretation" I would be tempted to reply that it was my intention to practise this form of "masturbation" by proxy on the therapist.

Other so-called "challenging measures" such as threatening to withdraw therapy unless the patient stops self-harming is crude, manipulative blackmail. This is hypocrisy considering that 'manipulation' often forms part of the symptom list of the psychiatric interpretation of self-harm.

"Attention-seeking"

What is attention-seeking? I know that I do not seek the degradation I have received in Accident and Emergency, neither do I want to be treated with sympathy nor pity. The only 'attention' I and others have sought at Accident and Emergency is treatment for our injuries. If I wanted 'attention' in an exhibitionist way, it would be much easier and pain-free to walk into the middle of the street and remove my clothes. I would not need to cut up my body. But if "attention" means being listened to and taken seriously, then along with the rest of the human race I'm attention-seeking.

Listening to a medical student friend talking about her secondment to Accident and Emergency she observed that self-harming patients were usually the quietest and most uncomplaining. That they only spoke when requested to.

A relative who works on maternity wards also observed that mothers who self-harm usually found it difficult to ask for support.

Sadly the myth of "attention-seeking" has resulted in people being categorised by stereotype.

Some service workers have been taught that self-harm is **always** "attention-seeking". This leads to the view that any expression of care/concern/empathy or compassion should be avoided at all costs. This would supposedly be interpreted as sympathy by the self-harmer. All self-harmers I have ever met have no desire to be an object of pity or sympathy. When compassion and respect are demonstrated **this** has a positive effect on self-worth. During cycles of self-harm, self-worth and care rapidly plummet, resulting in the individual feeling that she/he does not deserve anything good. When a professional shows respect this does raise the individuals' feelings of self-worth. Sometimes sufficiently to delay the next act of self-harm.

If you believe that self-harm is merely "attention-seeking" then consideration should be given to what attention that person needs. For some people self-harm is a form of communication to voice things that cannot be said. "Therapeutic" tools such as showing no emotion, giving no response, or being dismissive through to hostility in order to deter self-harm fails to demonstrate any success. Yet this philosophy continues.

Frequently, self-harming equates with being "bad" and managing not to harm equates to "good". Support may be dependant on the individual **not** self-harming. In other words - "good". So we may have to not be distressed in order to be seen as worthy of support. This is as logical as saying that a *"Depressive"* has to stop being depressed before counselling can start. It's almost as though self-harm is unbearable to see, hear or speak of.

I am not suggesting professionals should merely show us kindness. I am saying that there needs to be some respect, and self-harm is seen as a valid expression of distress. We are not stupid or silly. It is not merely a case of "pulling ourselves together".

This idea of "attention-seeking" has the effect of us being seen as "undeserving" patients. Labels such as, *"hysterical"*, *"histrionic"*, *"attention-seeking"* and *"acting out"* have historically been attached to women. It's a useful way of dismissing and negating them. It's also a cop-out for the professional. The labels have serious consequences; the severity of physical pain being questioned or ignored.

In addition to self-harm being viewed as "attention-seeking" there only appears to be three other interpretations. Self-harm is not in itself a described "disorder/syndrome/illness". The psychiatrist looks for an "underlying illness" to explain the behaviour. If an "underlying illness" is diagnosed then treatment of that condition goes ahead and self-harm gets neatly brushed under the carpet. It is seen as peripheral to the "illness".

Secondly, if no "underlying illness" is found (more likely if you are articulate), the individual may be described as having "nothing wrong", but that cutting/burning etc. is "abnormal".

Thirdly, if the clinician doesn't feel that he/she can get away with saying that there is nothing wrong with the individual. Or, that he/she doesn't know what category to put the patient into, the standby dustbin diagnoses are given; *"Personality Disorder"* or *"Behavioural Disorder"*.

These labels tend to be assigned to individuals whose patterns of distress do not 'fit' into any of the other psychiatric categorisations. People whose behaviour may be viewed as *"anti-social"* or *"deviant"*. Some psychiatrists view these pseudo conditions as being intractable to psychiatric help thereby giving the clinician a quick and easy way out of addressing the problem. Not co-operating with treatment, being *"difficult"* or disliked can lead to the diagnosis of *"personality disorder"*. It is the clinical term for arsehole. Frankly, it doesn't matter which interpretation is attached to you, they all ensure one thing. There is no meaningful discussion of the self harm. Self-harm is not seen as distress in its own right. Though one London teaching hospital now admits eating-distressed individuals who also self-harm in a direct, external way. They invented a label for it; *"Multi-Impulsive Bulimia"*. (How long can a label get?)The behaviourist approach does seem to be the more popular amongst professionals and yet so unhelpful to self-harmers. Professionals operating treatment programmes for eating distress are starting to realise how damaging behaviour modification is. One centre in Scotland has stated that it sees the 'casualties' of such treatments and has developed a radically different approach. As self-harm is not properly acknowledged it may take some time for the professionals to learn the same lesson with self-harmers.

Where self-harm fits into the criteria of "Danger to self" within the Mental

Health Act remains unclear. I have been Sectioned for hearing voices and for the assessment of "underlying illness". This seems crazy to me as my voices do not cause me to self-harm. Casualty officers may be told that self-harmers cannot be detained unless the injury was carried out with suicidal intent. This is not strictly true as a long record of self injury may colour the assessment of intent.

Self-injury without suicidal intent can be life-threatening or leave a permanent disability or disfigurement. So when does self-harm become a "Danger to Self"? The decision to Section is arbitrary. It is rarely for the reasons that it should be imposed according to the legal framework. People are rarely Sectioned for self-harm alone and if so, it tends to be done in the exercise of professionals covering themselves using the concept of "underlying illness" as the reason.

"You should trust us" is commonly heard in psychiatric and Accident and Emergency consulting rooms, but why should we? Why should anyone? Trust has to be earned, it cannot be assumed. Psychiatric workers need to understand that people who self-harm are used to rejection. We are rejected for our actions and therefore it becomes harder to trust or ask for help. We get the bureaucratic smack in the mouth, the write-off or abuse. Many professionals don't want to work with us. For those who do, you really need to let the individual know that you **want** to work with them, and that there will be a **commitment** to offer support regardless of the person harming or not. This cycle of rejection in psychiatric and medical services results in **"Cumulative Damage"**. This is where the individual becomes so used to direct and indirect negative responses that she/he becomes highly sensitised to any perceived negative expression. A filter bounces off everything positive and only lets through the negative. A facial expression is sufficient. Communication can be stopped by the drop of a phrase. It is important for professionals to be clear, direct and honest in their communication. Self-harmers have highly developed bull-shit detectors.

The parallel between animals in zoos and people in psychiatric hospitals is striking. Stereotypical behaviour can appear almost identical, even down to the look in the animal and human eyes. Animals will self-mutilate when placed in an unnatural and controlling environment with little stimulation or hope. This can happen to animals in single cages that defies the assertion that self -harm tends to be a *"learnt behaviour"*.

Acknowledging emotions as being real rather than "symptoms" causes psychiatry a problem. Anger and assertiveness are seen as something

47

dangerous in need of control. Professionals are often unwilling to listen to anger, particularly if that anger is related to treatment. The professional may feel it necessary to defend the indefensible rather than acknowledge flaws in the practice and logic of treatments. This leaves the patient with an impotent rage.

Expressions of pain (physical/emotional) can be equally ignored.

In Marc D. Feldman's paper, "The Challenge of Self-Mutilation: A Review.(Comprehensive Psychiatry vol. 29, no. 31988), He suggests that, *"Pain is often absent during the cutting; indeed, one may be able to suture the wounds without anaesthesia"*. **NO** one may not. I refute this. I have yet to meet someone who does not feel the pain of suturing. It is true that pain is frequently absent whilst injuring, sometimes there is no sensation. The pain of the injury may not be felt until a while afterwards but the long wait in casualty usually ensures that feeling has fully returned. Pain may be absent during injuring, the intensity of emotion is suppressing it. The body may possibly produce more of it's natural painkiller, endorphin. Alternatively, the individual may feel every bit of the pain whilst injuring. For me it varies according to other factors such as, area of the body, level of scar tissue, how bad I feel, whether I have eaten that day, time of my menstrual cycle. When I do feel pain I say to myself over and over, 'it doesn't matter, it doesn't matter', in order to deal with it. I get angry with myself for feeling the pain.

The degree and time of pain vary in individuals, but the pain of suturing is always felt. In individuals who harm themselves over many years there may be **more** pain involved in treatment as scar tissue does not respond so well to local anaesthetics and skin may become tight through loss of tissue.

Pain can be exacerbated by lack of medical care. A young friend of mine during her first psychiatric admission, inflicted a second degree burn which was not checked, let alone dressed. It is not therapeutic to place people at risk of infection. Emotional expressions of pain can also be ignored. Staff telling others to "stay way" from patient X as she was deemed to not be "worth it". Bereavement has been termed a "Grief Reaction" with crying ignored or observed. It is so lonely to cry and have someone watch you.

Professional fear or incompetence always becomes the patient's incompetence. Unlike Marks and Spencer, the customer is always wrong. One is supposed to agree to the spoken or unspoken contracts. Common statements made by psychiatrists include; "we can't stop you", "no one can stop you". Although this is practically true it's a negative stock response. A way of saying that 'you're on your own'. Maybe it is also a recognition that their therapies do not apply or their inability to look at it.

Continuing, persistent self-harm carries the assumption that everything must have been tried. Although people may have had extensive contact with psychiatric services, little time may have used to addressing the self-harm. Long records can walk into the consulting room before the patient does and that colours the psychiatrist's perceptions. Having worked in service provision with access to patient notes I am appalled at their inaccuracy and unreliability. The notes can appear like an exercise in character assassination . The wrong questions are asked and the doctor writes down his own answers. Contact between psychiatrists and self harmers will continue to be fruitless or confrontational until psychiatry surrenders it's assumptions.

Accident and Emergency

There is acknowledgement within the profession that personal moral judgement does affect clinical judgement.

The "Course book for medical sociology lectures and tutorials and family attachment scheme (2nd. Year students 1992/93) Department of general practice University of Sheffield. p. 21 contains the quote;

"A Criticism : Stigma in the organisation of casualty services.

Jeffrey studied the categorisations of patients by doctors working in casualty. Only some kinds of patients were allowed the full rights of the sick role. 'Good' patients were acutely ill, not responsible for their illness, and preferably in need of rapid treatment. 'Bad' or 'rubbish' patients were smelly, attempted suicides, or had 'trivial' complaints. These patients were 'taught a lesson' by being kept waiting, and possibly given uncomfortable treatment".

Accident and Emergency departments in inner cities are under considerable pressure and a waiting time of 7 to 8 hours for any patient is common. Accident and Emergency staff may feel that self-harming patients are an uneccessary drain on precious resources and a waste of time, particularly if they come regularly for treatment. Accident and Emergency is in a key position to make a difference to the course of a cycle of self-harm. Attending Accident and Emergency need not become another form of self- harm and there is a need for a co-ordinated response and policy. Department of Health guidelines make no distinction between self-harm and attempted suicide. Departments need to formulate their own.

If attending Accident and Emergency is negative 8 times out of 10, an individual may find it difficult to trust the staff on the other two occasions. This leaves the staff feeling frustrated by the suspicion of the self harmer. A positive example of intervention from an Accident and Emergency department is rare.

However Accident and Emergency Staff please note the following example;

> I was not expected to jump through the usual hoops of questions like "were you trying to kill yourself?" The necessary questions were not directed at me all in one go, I did not feel grilled. The overriding feeling that was communicated to me was one of care and concern, but not in a condescending way. My distress was acknowledged without judgement. Care was taken to ensure adequate pain relief. This reinforced that what had happened did really matter. I was treated like any other patient with dignity and respect. My physical privacy was respected too. I was not expected to show the doctor all my scars as others have demanded. The nurse held my hand whilst the anaesthetic was being injected. A most unusual occurrence. I was offered a bed on a general ward overnight, and I was not put under any pressure to see a psychiatrist or make promises that I could not keep. Usually, I would head straight for the door but on this occasion I felt able to accept their support because of the way it was offered. The sister visited me throughout the night, offering either to leave on my request or stay and listen to me if I felt able to talk.

Although offering a bed overnight would not always be appropriate or feasible, particularly in inner city hospitals, if it is possible, it can take the heat out of the individuals' situation. Giving a breathing space.

The Social Consequences of Self-Harm.

There are many medical/cosmetic and social consequences of self-harm. Scars are permanent and disfiguring. The scars have a negative effect on self-image, relationships and employment. People who are disfigured through self-injury are rarely asked by the health services how they feel about their disfigurement. It's as if it doesn't matter. It **does**. If a patient becomes disfigured through surgery or an accident they are offered counselling.

On the only occasion I tried to talk about the disfigurement with a psychiatric nurse She responded "Oh you'll have to learn to live with it". I know that, but it might have helped if I had been allowed to explore my feelings.

Cosmetic surgery for scars needs careful consideration. You need to consider why you really want it, is it for you, or is it to make other people feel better. You also need a sympathetic G.P. who will refer you to an N.H.S. plastic surgeon. You may have to wait a few months for an appointment. Your G.P. or the surgeon may not be prepared to do anything until you have been 'injury free' for a year, maybe even two. When you see the surgeon it is a good idea to take a friend or relative with you for moral support.

If "Scar Revision" (the removal of an area of scar tissue and resuturing), is a viable option and the surgeon is willing, there are further considerations. Be realistic about the outcome - the surgeon is unlikely to be able to take the scarring away completely. You may get a scar for a scar, but a much better looking one. You may have to wear a support bandage for a few months to aid the contraction of the wound. The results can be impressive, after a year you may really feel the difference. It can make a significant difference to contour defects(such as a large dent in a limb).

Camouflage make-up can also be effective in concealing the colour of injuries but does not affect contour defects. The Red Cross has trained cosmeticians to show you how. Your G.P. can refer you and most of the products are available on an N.H.S. prescription.

I had surgery on one arm and I still can see a significant difference. I truly believed I would never self-harm again. When I injured the same area, it was extremely difficult to accept. I felt ashamed. I tried the make-up but found applying it time consuming. I haven't been swimming or worn a sleeveless dress for 11 years, though sometimes I fantasise about it. I would like to think that one day I could walk out with a friend in a sleeveless dress and hold my head up and that I would be able to throw back any stares or comments. I would like to think that one day I would be able to reveal myself as a scarred woman and feel 'sod you, this is me and you have to accept me as I am'. 'Coming out' as a scarred person is not easy, we have the extra problem of being asked 'why?' as well as 'how?'.

Feelings about scars can vary, not everyone despises their scars. Some individuals may really need them as it may feel like the only tangible testimony of their pain, and may not want to conceal or remove them. There is no 'right 'or 'wrong' way to feel about your scars. How ever we feel is justified.

For some women being scarred, especially to the breasts, can have an affect on femininity and sexuality. There can be androgynous feelings and fear that potential partners may reject them. It is important to talk about fears with a partner preferably before the relationship becomes sexual. Look at ways of putting us at ease, i.e. no or low lighting, being semi-dressed to start with etc. With care and sensitivity, a scarred person's confidence can increase.

The medical consequences of self-harm have included not being taken seriously or being given the necessary priority for treatment for other conditions. I experienced discrimination a few years ago when I needed an operation and the consultant made all kinds of assumptions about me because of my self-harm. He assumed that I would bang my head against the wall after surgery and consequently wasn't keen to do it. Other members of his team

51

who knew me had made no such assumption and talked him into seeing me earlier than he might.

Another social consequence of self-harm is unemployment. Loss of an offer of employment is almost automatic when an employer requires a medical or a uniform reveals the scars. Health Authorities are amongst the worst offenders for discrimination and as far as I'm aware no employer in the country includes mental health in their Equal Opportunities Policy. There are many pro's and cons to lying, it depends on what kind of work it is. The decision has to reflect what the individual can handle. On different occasions, I have lied or have been honest. I lied when I undertook training in operating theatres. That did prove to be stressful, as I was always afraid of being 'found out' which could have resulted in instant dismissal. When I have been honest, it has been for work in mental health and I presented it as something positive that I could use in my work. I did get the job.

It's a difficult judgement to make, and has now been made much more difficult with the recommendations of the Clothier Report in response to the implications of Beverly Allitt's conviction. This report will carry serious consequences for the nursing profession, and for nurses and patients who self-harm.

The Clothier report recommendations include;

"No one with evidence of a major personality disorder should be employed in the profession"

"Further consideration should be given to proposals that any nursing applicant with excessive absence through sickness, excessive use of counselling or medical facilities, or self-harming behaviours such as attempted suicide, self-laceration or eating disorder, should not be accepted for training until they have shown the ability to live without professional support and have been in stable employment for at least two years".

"Consideration should be given to a scheme asking G.P.'s, with the applicants consent, to certify that those wanting to work in the N.H.S. were medically suitable".

This is an ill-conceived knee-jerk response, and has not responded to the factors that led to Beverly Allitt being able to commit such atrocities for so long. It has merely listed her alleged problems as undesirable attributes for nurses and nurse training candidates to possess. To suggest that people who self-harm are more likely to harm others is objectionable. There is no evidence to back this ridiculous assertion. I have known nurses who have self-harmed or had an eating disorder. Their personal difficulties have often made them better nurses and role models for students. The gap in training and support combined with the Clothier report leaves nurses who have had or develop a self-injury problem only able to continue their careers by remaining silent. Seeking help will be to their detriment. I am saddened that a nurse of many years experience was suspended from Ms Allitt's hospital due to a past incident of self-harm being discovered, and that a student nurse was dismissed from training on seeking help for his problem last year. If the nursing profession is going to be 'mental health policed', how many people will be seen as healthy enough to enter or remain in nursing. Just how 'sane' and problem -free will you have to be? This kind of health fascism highlights the abuse and inadequacies in services that face patients who self-harm. Therefore, if nurses are to be punished or excluded for self-harm, what hope does that give people who self harm walking into Accident and Emergency feeling terrified and misunderstood?

Alternatives

Bringing together people with direct experience helps to smash the isolation that many of us feel. The first self-harm newsletter in the country has been published by the Bristol support group. Getting realistic funding for survivor-led research will require much effort on the part of survivors and their allies. The Bristol Crisis Service For Women has undertaken a 2 year research project to research womens experiences of self-harm and treatment and this will be an important support for the currently ignored views and criticisms. Although womens/user groups already know the extent of bad practice, we need the statistical data to back up our fight for political action and demands for change.

Many of us would like to see user-led/run crisis services, where there is a phone number available to call 24 hours a day, 7 days a week. Where someone can come to see us at a time of crisis and offer support at home, or talk over the phone. The Bristol Crisis Service For Women operates the only phone line in the country with a specific service for women who self-harm. There is a clear need for self-harm help-lines in every city. Many of us want access to short term sanctuary without diagnosis/'treatment'/drugs/Sections. Houses with 'rage' facilities (a room to smash things in), where people can go without going through exhausting admission procedures. Everyone may need access to this, not just those of us who seriously self-harm. We all have explosive feelings that need to be let go to stop them from going bad.

There is a need for advocacy in Accident and Emergency departments, particularly when an individual finds it hard to ask someone to accompany them, or there is no one to ask. Medical, mental health, and citizen advocacy schemes should include self-harm as part of their services. The Samaritans can play a role.

Staff training and support by people with direct experience will help consciousness raising. 'De-training' health workers will assist to change attitudes and perceptions. The role the medical services play causing and continuing the need to self-harm must be recognised. There needs to be non-medical alternatives.

Counselling services have noticed an increase in self-harm and eating distress amongst undergraduates. This is hardly surprising considering the increasingly intolerable stress that students now face; homelessness, massive debt, and the possibility of unemployment after graduation. It is sad that we live in a society where stress is turned back on ourselves. It is an indictment of our repressive society.

Points for people who self-harm

1) Find some one you feel safe with to talk to.

2) If you need treatment at hospital for your injuries try taking someone with you for moral support. You are less likely to be badly treated if you have someone in the cubicle with you. If your friends feel unable to assist you here try approaching an advocacy service or the Samaritans.

3) Start a mutual support group, you are not alone, and it will help to share your feelings with people who have been through it. Your local MIND association should be able to offer to you logistic support such as finding a venue to meet, photocopying posters. Take posters to Accident and Emergency, Rape Crisis, womens groups, etc. Accident and Emergency departments are usually more than willing to display a poster. Make contact with other groups across the country(listed at the back of this book), for advice and support. When you meet, discuss what kind of group you want to have, i.e. closed or open, women only or mixed. In my experience the only essential ground rule needed is that there should be an agreement to never self-harm on the group's premises. You will also need a contact point for enquiries such as a PO BOX no, or the local MIND association. Don't be surprised if you get a therapist contacting you offering to lead the group and "cure" you! It is difficult for people to come forward and the group may take some time to establish but don't lose heart. Even if it doesn't continue to meet but you keep in contact with one another it would have been worth it.

4) Carry a "Crisis card". Crisis Cards will become available from Survivors Speak Out (address at the back of the book). If you experience crises that bring

you into contact with hospital services, a crisis card is useful. On the card you can name someone to contact who can act as your advocate and a list of what is and isn't helpful for you. There is no guarantee that your wishes will be respected; Crisis cards are not legally binding but are worth using.

5) Have a first-aid kit. If your injuries do not require hospital treatment, or, you feel that you can no longer face visiting Accident and Emergency, using a first-aid kit will minimise the risk of infection. Use a clean implement when you injure, to minimise infection. If you do not have a knowledge of first-aid, a basic First-Aid course run by the Red Cross or St. Johns Ambulance is a good idea.

6) Take a course in Assertiveness, something many people benefit from generally.

7) Try to identify factors/feelings/perceptions that lead to self-harm, and see if it's possible for you with helper/s to intervene at an earlier stage.

8) Look at what might limit the damage you do to yourself, i.e. how and when you harm yourself.

9) Look at how you deal with anger and tension. If these feelings lead to self-harm consider ways of letting off steam regularly which are not harmful i.e. going to a field to scream.

10) Don't punish yourself if you've harmed yourself after a period of not harming. Tomorrow's another day. Think of what you have achieved.

Suggestions for relatives/friends

1) Don't reject us, we really need your acceptance of the self-harm.

2) Don't give ultimatums - 'do this or...'. There are no easy answers.

3) If able offer to go to Accident and Emergency with the individual to give moral support. You can act as an advocate.

4) Do not assume that when a person is **not** self-harming that they do not need support.

5) Don't give up, especially when the medical services have.

Suggestions for psychiatric/counselling services

1) Abandon your assumptions and change Your priorities from diagnosis - treatment to; a) Listen b) Seek out the person's own knowledge. c) Act on that information. d) Take the person seriously.

2) Re-evaluate your concepts by being prepared to learn from your client. When was the last time you listened to them for 20 minutes uninterrupted?

3) Don't dispute a persons reality, acknowledge it.

4) Emotional blackmail doesn't work in the long term.

5) Be prepared to offer support whilst different strategies are tried. During that time self-harm may continue. You can't go from A-Z overnight. Consider damage-limitation strategies in combination with the reasons and how do we get her/him to stop.

6) Offer occasional sanctuary without restrictive measures or pressure to take drugs. Find out what the individual needs and would accept when there is no crisis, it is hard to state needs whilst in crisis.

7) Make admission for the maintenance of safety easier. Perhaps a letter that can be taken to Accident and Emergency may bridge the communication problems. Admission procedures add to the distress. Being asked endless lists of questions, many of which are irrelevant is stressful. Does it really matter whether a person can count backwards from 100 taking away 7 each time or not? (can you?)

8) Don't concentrate on how many times a person self-harms, celebrate each time it is evaded.

9) Forget behaviourist approaches - there is no impartial evidence that they work.

10) Gender stereotyping needs to be monitored. For example, a female self-harmer being told, "[Your condition is because]... you're a typical woman" is unacceptable.

11) Involve people with personal experience in staff training and policy. Encourage staff to explore their own self-harm.

Rights for self-harmers within Accident and Emergency departments and suggestions for Accident and Emergency staff

When I have led training sessions for general or psychiatric student nurses they tell me self-harm is not properly covered in their training. Students often feel frightened and do not know how to respond. The involvement of people with personal experience in training is vital. Survivor trainers are available from support groups, Survivors Speak Out, MindLink, and the Bristol Crisis Service for Women. (Addresses are contained in the resource list)

Once qualified there is usually little hope of staff receiving support and exploring their self-awareness. This exploration is imperative to better communication and understanding of prejudice.

1) Any necessary medical treatment for self-inflicted injuries should be a right. Moral judgement should not affect clinical judgement. Treatment should not be dependent upon the individual agreeing to psychiatric intervention.

2) A patient with self-inflicted injuries has same right as other patients; the right not to have students observing or treating.

3) Pain relief should be given the same priority as any other patient. Withholding anaesthesia as a punishment or deliberately giving inadequate anaesthesia is unethical and will only result in further loss of self-worth in the patient. Often leading to further harm.

4) Judgement, annoyance and simplistic solutions or lectures will not deter a person from self-harming. It will make more work for you.

5) Don't guilt-trip the individual for seeking treatment for an injury.

6) Don't write people off, especially those with a long history of self harm.

7) Try not to give the impression that you don't care and that you merely have to ascertain whether there is suicidal intent.

8) It is okay to say to the individual that you don't understand, feel frustrated or helpless. We would rather you were open about these feelings. We will know if you are feeling them anyway.

9) Basic human comfort is underestimated, it takes little time or effort. A comforting touch may be quite beneficial and help to alleviate physical tension, especially when most of the contact the individual may have with their own body is negative or painful.

10) Try not to launch straight into standard mental state examination questions. Ask how that person's day has been. Try to engage the person in conversation not related to their injuries.

11) Show that the self harm does matter and acknowledge the person's distress even if you don't understand it.

12) Don't force a person to talk if she/he feels unable to. Statements like "If you

don't talk to us we can't help you" will not encourage a person to talk. The individual has to be reassured that their distress will be taken seriously.

13) Encourage the patient to talk about previous responses and don't feel that you have to justify bad treatment. Acknowledge our feelings and if appropriate offer information about complaints procedures.

14) Consider your body language and how you speak. We usually feel very small and frightened therefore you could easily intimidate us.

15) Never talk about us in the third person. Try not to whisper to colleagues then speak in a loud voice to us. Say everything either clearly within earshot or completely out of earshot. Half-heard conversations feed suspicion.

16) Don't physically humiliate us by leaving us half naked or demanding to see all our scars. Disfigured self-harmers require the same sensitivity as patients who are disfigured through surgery or accident.

17) If you have the time, even 10 minutes, listen. Invite the individual to come in and talk to whoever they may feel able to approach even when there isn't an injury. Devise an accessible, workable system for this.

18) Ask how safe the person feels, if there is the availability and if it is late at night and it is a person you are seeing frequently offer a bed overnight on a general or observation ward. It can the heat out of the situation.

19) Refusal of psychiatric treatment does not necessarily equal no desire to stop self-harming. Find out what local voluntary/womens organisations have to offer. See if there are any counselling services that have an interest in self-injury. See where the nearest support is.

20) Forget your assumptions. How do YOU define self-harm? If you see a colleague being abusive, challenge them, don't walk away.

21) Consult people who self-harm when formulating a policy for your department. It is possible to get their services through mental health user/survivor groups or the local MIND association.

22) Self-harm is distressing for staff and students to see. Support and training are essential.

23) Don't give up. People do survive self-harm even after many years.

Final Cut.

Within these walls
Sits my soul
Staring at me
In stifled
Strangled
Silence.

Where are you/me?
Muted resonance replies.

Within these walls
Life and Humanity
Is ratified by my ragged flesh,
By the bloody blade
Tearing,
Disfeaturing,
My mutated frame.

Within these walls
There is a holocaust
Crying tears of blood,
Living on the razors edge
Waiting,
For the final cut.

Sometimes...

Sometimes ...   all I can feel is the warmth of my blood
running away from my body.

Sometimes...   all I can feel is the searing pain
of your disgust and rejection.

Sometimes...   all I want to do is cut myself into tiny pieces
and throw me all away.

Sometimes...   all I want is someone to hold me
when I can't hold onto myself.

Sometimes...   all I think is the next cut must be enough.

Sometimes...   all I think is,'It doen't matter, it doesn't matter'.

Sometimes...   all I can feel is the needle in my flesh,
wanting the pain to stop,
thinking where will my spirit rest?

RESOURCE LIST

Organisations for people who self-injure

Bristol Crisis Service for Women

BCSW is a collectively run charity set up in 1986 to respond to the needs of women in emotional distress. They have a particular focus on self-injury and provide a national help-line for women in distress, on Friday and Saturday evenings from 9pm to 12.30am on 0117 9251119

They offer any woman who rings a chance to talk through her feelings in confidence, without fear of being judged or dismissed. They also support self-help groups, offer training, and publish a wide range of literature.

For further information and a publications listing contact:

BCSW
P.O. BOX 654
Bristol BS99 1XH

National Self-Harm Network

The NSHN is a survivor-led organisation committed to campaign for the Rights and understanding of people who self-injure. The network is focused on its campaign to improve the treatments in Accident & Emergency departments, publishing leaflets for health staff, supporters and people who self-injure.

Contact:

Louise Pembroke NSHN
c/o Survivors Speak Out
34 Osnaburgh Street
London NW1 3ND

42nd Street

42nd Street is a mental health service for young people aged fifteen to twenty-five (in Manchester) who face wide and varied problems including self-harm and suicide. They offer a variety of individual support alongside a range of groups based at the resource, and within the local community.

They have initiated specific projects, including a suicide/self-harm project which itself offers individual and group support to young people.

They completed a research project on young people, self-harm and suicide and produced an excellent book based on their findings. Contact;

Suicide/Self-Harm worker.
42nd Street
2nd Floor, Swan Buildings
20 Swan Street
Manchester M4 5JW
Telephone: 0161 8320170

Newsletters

SHOUT (Self-harm overcome by understanding and tolerance)

SHOUT is a bi-monthly newsletter which aims to breakdown isolation and provide support for women affected by self-harm. (will accept subscriptions from men too). It is read and contributed to by women all over the country, by groups and by professionals who work with people affected by self-harm.

SHOUT includes: articles, pen-pals/contacts, letters, poems, cartoons, book reviews, plus details of help-lines, groups and resources.

To subscribe to SHOUT contact:

SHOUT
c/o P.O. BOX 654
Bristol BS99 1XH
(The mailing list is confidential and copies will be sent in a plain envelope)

The Cutting Edge - A newsletter for women living with self-inflicted violence.

This is a forum for women who live with SIV and their friends.

To subscribe contact:

The Cutting Edge
P.O. BOX 20819
Cleveland
Ohio 44120
U.S.A.

WAVES - Women making waves about abuse

A bi-monthly newsletter for women who have experienced abuse of any kind in childhood, and their supporters.

To subscribe contact:

WAVES
c/o 82 Colston Street
Bristol BS1 5BB
(The mailing list is confidential and WAVES is sent in an unmarked envelope)

Pen-friend Network
SASH- Survivors of Abuse and Self-harming

Pen-friend network which offers support, friendship on a one to one basis in writing.

Contact:

SASH
20 Lackmore Road
Enfield
Middlesex EN1 4PB

Contact one of the following for information about self-harm support groups which may be available in your area:

Bristol Crisis Service for Women

SHOUT newsletter

Your local MIND association, mental health user/survivor group or women's centre.

Self-Harm Training for Statutory and Voluntary sector agencies and professionals

Experienced trainers with first-hand experience of self-injury are available from the following organisations:

National Self Harm Network

(see earlier for address)

MINDlink

MIND
Granta House
15-19 Broadway
Stratford
London E15 4BQ

ASHES - Abuse and self-harm, experience of survival

Training on self-harm and sexual abuse issues. Training packages offered.

Contact:

Diane

0117 9711844

Basement Project

The Basement Project provides training, consultation, supervision, groups, workshops and publications for individuals and those working in community and mental health services.

Their work is founded on respect for individuals and their rights to determine their own needs and make choices for themselves.

Contact:

Lois Arnold
The Basement Project
82 Colston Street
Bristol BS1 5BB

Mental Health Organisations

User/Survivor organisations (contact these organisations for details of local user/survivor groups)

Survivors Speak Out

A network of mental health system survivors, groups and allies.

34 Osnaburgh Street
London NW1 3ND
Telephone: 0171 9165472

Hearing Voices Network

A network of people who hear voices.

C/O Creative Support
Fourways House
16 Tariff Street
Manchester M1 2EP
Telephone: 0161 2283896

UKAN (UK Advocacy Network)

A co-ordinating network for user-led advocacy groups.

Room 302
Premier House
14 Cross Street
Sheffield S1 2HG

MINDlink

MIND's consumer network

(see earlier for address)

Survivors' Poetry

Publications, workshops and performances by and for mental health system survivors.

34 Osnaburgh Street
London NW1 3ND
Telephone: 0171 9165317

Scottish Users' Network

Network for mental health service users in Scotland.

40 Shandwyck Place
Edinburgh

Us Network

National federation of service users in Wales.

C/o Wales MIND
23 St Mary Street
Cardiff CF1 2AA

Mental Health - General Information
MIND

Granta House
15-19 Broadway
Stratford
London E15 4BQ
Information telephone line: 0181 5221728
(MIND publishes a leaflet entitled "Understanding Self-Harm")

Sexual Abuse Organisations

Survivors Network (Sussex)

Self-help groups and forums for women survivors of sexual abuse. Newsletter for members.

Contact:

P.O. BOX 188
Brighton BN1 7JW

FAMAC (Dumbarton)

Female Adults Molested as Children

Provides group support for women who were abused as children, or who are mothers or carers of children who have been abused.

Contact:

Hilda McLaughlin

01389 752238

Phone-line: Tuesdays 7-9pm.

Breaking Free

Supports women survivors of child sex abuse (18yrs+)

Contact:

Samantha Rowe
c/o Flat 2
66 Cheam Road
Sutton
Surrey
SMI 2SU
Telephone: 0181 7707533

NSPCC

Free 24hr help-line for abused children, families and survivors. Has information on local resources.

Telephone: 0800 800500

Childline

24hr help-line for children and teenagers.

Telephone: 0800 1111

Survivors

A men's self-help group that is the only national support organisation working with any male victim or survivor of sexual violence. They also run a telephone help-line on Mon, Tues and Weds 7-10pm.

P.O. BOX 2470
London W2 1NW
Help-line: 0171 8333737

Rape Organisations

Rape Crisis Centres will help women and girls who have survived sexual violence and abuse and are often run by women survivors. You will find your local centre by looking in the telephone directory or contact:

London Rape Crisis Centre
P.O. BOX 69
London WC1X 9NJ
Crisis Help-line Mon-Fri 6-10pm: Sat-Sun 10am-10pm 0171 8371600

Women Against Rape

Counselling, legal advice and support for women who have been raped or assaulted. Contact:

71 Tonbridge Street
London WC1H 9DZ
Telephone: 0171 8377509

Women's Organisations
Women's Aid Federation

Advice, help and information for women suffering from domestic violence. Contact:

P.O. BOX 391
Bristol BS99 7WS
Telephone: 01179 633494
Help-line: 00117 9633542

Women's Therapy Centre

Services for survivors of sexual abuse and training for workers. Face to face counselling and groups. Contact:

6-9 Manor Gardens
London N7 6LA
Telephone Mon-Fri 2-4pm 0171 2817879

Threshold

Initiative for women and mental health. Organises conferences, self-help groups, and offers some face to face counselling. Produces a newsletter. Contact:

14 St Georges Place
Brighton
East Sussex BN1 4GB
Telephone: 01273 626444

WISH - Women in Special Hospitals and Secure Units.

Contact:

25 Horsell Road
London N5 1XL
Telephone: 0171 7006684
Look in your local telephone directory for details of your local Women's Centres/Resource centres

Eating Distress Organisations
Eating Disorders Association

Offers support and advice to sufferers of Anorexia and Bulimia and their family and friends. Also offers a national network of self-help groups, contact addresses, bi-monthly newsletter and have a book-list and mailing service. Contact:

Sackville Place
44-48 Magdalene Street
Norwich
Norfolk NR3 1JE
Help-line Mon-Fri 9am-6.30pm 0191 2210233

Northern Initiative on Women and Eating

Offers a telephone contact point at which women can talk, perhaps for the first time, about their use of food and how this makes their lives difficult. They can get information about local and national service provision for eating problems and related issues.

Also, group work for women, to support them in exploring their eating problems and opportunities for change. Groupworkers do not give advice or tell women what to do. And open support sessions for women, on a weekly basis.

Training offered to other workers supporting people with eating difficulties. Contact:

1 Pink Lane
Newcastle-upon-Tyne NE1 5DW
Telephone: 0191 2210233

Young People
Youth Access

Offers free confidential information and advice to young people under 26 and holds a directory of youth counselling services all over the country. Contact:

1-2 Taylors Yard
67 Alderbrook Road
London SW12 8AE
Telephone: 0181 7729900

42nd Street

(see earlier for address)

Offcentre

Free confidential counselling for survivors of self-harm and sexual abuse. Male and female 13-25yrs, living, working or studying in Hackney. Survivors group for women currently running. Contact:

Hackney Young Peoples Counselling Service
25 Hackney Grove
London E8
Telephone: 0181 9858566

Counselling
British Association for Counselling

Information on counselling and therapy. Can provide list of local contacts.

Send S.A.E. to:

1 Regent Place
Rugby
Warwickshire CV21 2PJ

Disfigurement

Disfigurement Guidance Centre

Offers support to patients and their families, advice on camouflage and natural aid techniques and acts as an information and research centre. Contact:

P.O. BOX 7

Cupar

Fife KY15 4PF

Telephone: 01337 870281

Changing Faces

Provides information, individual help and support to all those directly or indirectly affected by disfigurement. Contact:

1-2 Junction Mews
London W2 1PN
Telephone: 0171 7064232

Plastic surgery information

British Association of Plastic Surgeons

Royal College of Surgeons
35-43 Lincolns Inn Fields
London WC2A 3PN

Rights

If you want to have access to your medical notes, make a complaint about access to services, or actual treatment (such as attitude or refusal of treatment on the grounds of self-infliction)then contact your local Community Health Council for advice and information. Your local phone directory will list their number. You can also complain in writing directly to the Chief Executive or the Complaints Manager of a hospital Trust. The hospital switchboard will give the names and address to write to. Likewise, you can contact the Access to Health Records manager directly and request an application form.

Please let the National Self Harm Network know if you are refused medical treatment on the grounds of self-infliction or are subjected to punitive treatments, the network is monitoring these practices.

For legal advice concerning psychiatric treatment contact:

MIND Legal Information Line on Mon/Wed/Fri 2-4.30pm 0181 5192122 ext:284

NHS and Voluntary sector services for people who self-injure

<u>Crisis Recovery Unit</u>

An in-patient unit for individuals who persistently self-harm. Takes country wide referrals.

For further enquiries contact:

Barbara Vaughan
Ward Administrator
Fitzmary 1
Bethlam Royal Hospital
Monks Orchard Road
Beckenham
Kent BR3 3BX
Telephone: 0181 7764273

Nationally, there are very few services for people who self-injure. Ask your GP to find out what services exists in your area. (Some health professionals including psychotherapists are reluctant to offer support to people who self-injure.)

Accident & Emergency departments may have a "psychiatric liaison nurse", available Monday to Friday, 9-5pm. They are available to people attending A &E with self-injury. Other departments may also have " deliberate self-harm" social workers attached to the department, again, usually during office hours. These professionals may offer a few counselling sessions or referrals. If you wish to see one of these, inform the Triage nurse when you arrive at A & E.

Crisis intervention services and "Crisis houses" vary widely. Many areas are covered by neither. Crisis intervention services are usually run by Health Authorities and are multi-disciplinary (i.e. Psychiatrist, Approved Social Worker, GP).

Crisis houses which offer short-term admission as an alternative to psychiatric hospital admission are run by voluntary and statutory agencies but vary in their approach to and acceptance of people who self-injure. Be aware, some projects require individuals to adhere to a "contract" whereby the individual promises not to injure themselves. Failure to comply has resulted in some people having all support withdrawn and asked to leave. It is best to ask about the policy on self-injury before using any service.

There are some local mental health help-lines, check your local phone directory. Help-lines can be good at times of crisis. A very few even offer a Free-Phone number. When all else fails, the Samaritans are available 24hrs a day on: 0345 909090

Recommended Reading

Fed up and Hungry - Women, Oppression and Food.
Marilyn Lawrence, Editor. (The Women's Press).

The Beauty Myth - Naomi Wolf (Vintage).

Eating Distress - Perspectives from personal experience.
Louise Roxanne Pembroke, Editor. (Survivors Speak Out).

Toxic Psychiatry - Peter R. Breggin M.D. (Fontana).

On Our Own - a compelling case for patient-controlled mental
health services. (MIND publications).

Accepting Voices - a new analysis of the experience of hearing
voices outside the illness model. (MIND publications).

Self-help alternatives to mental health services - Vivien Lindow
(MIND publications).

Purchasing mental health services: self-help alternatives - Vivien
Lindow (MIND publications)

Stopovers on my way home - a journey into the psychiatric
survivor movement in the U.S.A, Britain and the Netherlands -
Mary O'Hagan (Survivors Speak Out).

Survivor's Poetry - from dark to light. An illustrated anthology -
(Survivors Press).

Users and Abusers of Psychiatry - Lucy Johnstone (Routledge).

Women's Madness - misogyny or mental illness - Jane Ussher
(Harvester Wheatsheaf).

Shrink Resistant - the struggle against psychiatry in Canada -
Bonnie Burstow and Don Weitz, Editors (New Star Books -
Vancouver).

Printed in the United Kingdom
by Lightning Source UK Ltd.
112654UKS00001B/160